ROBINSON DESTRUCTION BOOK 2

KATHI S. BARTON

This is a work of fiction. Names, characters, places, and incidents are products of the author's imagination or are used fictitiously and are not to be construed as real. Any resemblance to actual events, locations, organizations, or persons, living or dead, is entirely coincidental.

World Castle Publishing, LLC
Pensacola, Florida
Copyright © Kathi S. Barton 2019
Paperback ISBN: 9781950890774
eBook ISBN: 9781950890781
First Edition World Castle Publishing, LLC, September 23, 2019
http://www.worldcastlepublishing.com

Cover: Karen Fuller
Editor: Maxine Bringenberg

Chapter 1

Anna didn't know what to do with the man who acted like he was fucking attached to her hip. Every time she moved, just to get up and move to the bathroom, he'd be right there with her, helping her into a panic attack. Not really, but that was what it felt like to her. Finally having enough, she stopped and turned to look at him.

"Don't you have anything else that you can be doing? I don't even care if you go outside and play with yourself. Just leave me alone." He grinned at her. "You're not all that charming, if that is what you're going for. I have crushed bigger bugs than you."

"What is it about me that has you on edge?" She asked him how long he had to listen to her answer. "Okay, that was mean, but I'm thinking that's your normal way of talking to people. By the way, I've gotten you an extension on your classes you're taking. I don't want you to be missing out on anything while you're here."

"What I'd really like to do is gather up my shit and get

the hell out of town." He told her that he'd be going with her. "I don't want you around at all, much less you going with me someplace. Did you read over that report that I got from Rogen? It tells you all the reasons that you should be running from me. Not spending all your time here with me. I'm a grown assed woman, and I don't need you here holding my hand."

"I don't think that I'd offer you my hand. You'd more than likely bite it off." She growled at him. "I'm not sure if you feel the same way I do about me growling at you, but all it does when you do it is make me want to spread you out before me and lick every square inch of you."

"You're not helping." He nodded and sat down after helping her to the bed again. "Why are you here? Really? There isn't any reason at all for you to be sitting around like a puppy with your tongue handing out."

"Your brother Noah, or I guess you call him Junior, is out of prison." That nearly had her falling to the floor. Had Morgan not been there to catch her, she would have ended up spread out anyway, without anything at all sexual about it. "I'm here until we can figure out where he's headed. Well, I say that like I have any idea what I'd have to do to find him. But Rogen is doing it. She's also trying to figure out how he got released."

"I call him that because he absolutely hates being called Junior, now that he has a record. So, he's been hating it since he was about seventeen, I guess. Was Junior released or did he escape? Is that what you're telling me?" Morgan said that was one of the things that Rogen was working on. "I guess I should have figured that he'd be out soon. I'd forgotten to keep up with his prison term. My father is who I've been the most worried about. Him and my brothers David and Bud."

"Junior has a watch dog on him right now. As soon as Rogen was made aware of Junior being released, she put someone on all three of them. Your father, he's bitching about his health and that the jail is making him lose weight. He needs it, but that's beside the point for him, I think. He needs to lose weight, but not because of anything that they're doing. He's eating himself into a stupor. I think Rogen said that he weighs nearly four hundred pounds now." Anna asked him how she'd know shit like that. "It's her job to know all kinds of shit. And some shit that I don't even question her about."

"She didn't strike me as the type that would be a coffee girl to anyone." Morgan laughed and said that she'd be the one demanding the coffee. If she drank it. "My father, does she think that he'll be getting out anytime soon?"

"She didn't say, but I'd not count on it. Now that he's on her fucking list — her words, not mine — he's not going to fart unless she knows about it before he does. I didn't ask her what that was supposed to mean. Rogen scares me in ways that I had to tell you about. She's a real ball buster. Much, I'm sure, as you are." Anna told him that she wasn't that, but someone that had been knocked around more than most. "I believe you. Rogen also pulled up your records for hospital visits, as well as other things."

"What does it matter anyway?" Morgan asked her what she meant. "You've already decided that I'm not mate material for you. Just look at you. You're sitting here in a pair of jeans that cost more than I make at my job. Or the job that I did have. He told me that if I missed a single day, he'd fire me. Then there are your shoes. What did you pay for them? More than two hundred bucks, I'm sure."

7

"Not that I understand what the price of my clothing has to do with you not being mate material, but I'll tell you. My parents bought me the jeans for Christmas last year. I've not had a chance to wear them as yet, because I've been working harder than I should have taking over another man's classes at the college. Not to say that I didn't enjoy them, but it was taking up a great deal of my time. The shoes? I have no idea who gave them to me. I'm thinking that it was Jonas, as he and I have the same sized feet. But as they were still in the box and had the tags on them, I can only assume that he didn't like the fit of them and gave them to me." She looked away. "Don't do that, Anna. Just let me explain some things to you. I have money. A good deal of it, as a matter of fact. I'm a dean at the college, and I've never been one to spend a great deal of money on anything unless I really need it. Even then it had better have several uses, as well as last me long enough that I feel I got my money's worth."

"I don't have shit." He said that he knew that. "Rogen again, I'm assuming. Why is she so hot on finding out what there is to know about me? As I've mentioned to you before, I'm not mate material to you."

Before she could think that he was going to move, he was over her, his legs on either side of her own. His hands held hers above her head, and he was looking down at her with such hunger that the need to look away from him was overwhelming. But she couldn't do it.

"Every time I look at you, all I can think about is seeing you large with our child. I have no idea why that thought keeps occupying my mind, but it does. To imagine you naked in my arms, another thought that I keep having, is almost more than I can take and still not touch you." He put both her hands into his one larger one and brushed his hand over her cheek. "You feel as soft as you look. The kiss from yesterday only makes me want more of you. To taste all that you have to offer. However, I won't take unless you consent. As for not being mate material, I can only hope that I'm a better mate to you than you think you will be for me."

He got off her then, her body suddenly feeling bereft of his warmth. Without saying a word, he sat down in the chair he'd been in and watched her. Anna had never wanted to cry so badly in her life. Looking at him, she let the tears flow while she told him off.

"You're a big man, aren't you? Did you think to scare me into submission? Well, it won't work. I'm made of stronger shit than you are, buster, and if you try that again, they'll be wiping up your body for the next twenty years or so." He asked her if she felt better. "Better? Hell no, I don't feel better. I fucking hurt. And I'm terrified that I'm going to fucking fall in love with you and you'll leave me to the wolves, so to speak, when you've had your fill. I know nothing about you other than what you've deemed it necessary for me to know. But you know everything there is to know about me, including, I'm sure, how much money I owe on my rent, which is overdue, as well as my college loans."

He didn't say anything as he sat there for a few minutes. But he did stand up and tell her that Rogen was coming to see her. As he went to the door, he paused for a moment and looked at her. She could see his anger, and wanted to shield herself from it. Instead, she lifted her chin up to show him that she didn't care what he did to her.

"Your student loans were paid off as of this morning. As my mate and with me being the dean at the college, they waived those from their books. I didn't do that. Someone in the offices found out and did it for you. Rogen paid up your rent so that your place would be there should you'd rather live there than in the home that I have for us both. I had nothing to do with that either." Anna started to tell him to not do anything for her. "I'm leaving now. Not because I want to, but because you're upset and saying things that you might regret later, though I highly doubt it."

The door closed behind him and Anna laid there. If she'd been able to get up and go after him, she would have. Anna didn't like that he'd had the last word. Sitting up in the bed a little more, she looked around the room. It just occurred to her that she had a better room here than she did at home. Not to mention anytime she pulled the nurse call cord, someone was in there almost as soon as she put the handheld call thing down.

"Hello." She looked at Rogen and asked her what the hell she was doing there. "Still in a shitty mood, I see. Morgan asked me to come by and give you this."

The thick file was tossed in her lap. It might well have hurt, it was that heavy, but she'd been healing more every day. Picking it up, she asked Rogen what it was. Instead of telling her what was in it, Rogen told her to open it and read it.

Opening the file cover, there was a picture of Morgan. She'd bet anything that it was his license picture. The man even took great license pictures. Anna would bet that anything he did, he'd be perfect at it.

"You mentioned to him that you knew nothing about him. So he had me do a thorough check on him, then print it up and hand it over. Some of the things in there, I'm sure even he's not aware of. Or, more than likely, doesn't care about." Anna laid it down. "You can read it or not. I could care less. But you pissed off one of the nicest men that I've ever known. I don't know whether I should punch you in the face for it or congratulate you for getting under his skin. I'm leaning toward the punch, just so you know."

"Why?" Rogen asked her what she meant. "Why did he have you gather this up? I didn't mean for him to give me a whole rundown on his life."

"Didn't you? I don't know you that well, mostly because you've been pushing us all away since the moment you opened your eyes. But you don't strike me as being one that trusts easily. Nor do you seem to think you have much reason to say you're sorry, or to thank someone. Am I right?" She nodded at Rogen. "Yeah, I thought so. In addition to having this all gathered for you, Morgan also had me add you to all his accounts. To put your name on the deed to his home, as well as the beneficiary line to his life insurance policy. Including the one that the university takes out on him."

"Again, why would he do that?" Rogen shrugged. "You know. Don't give me that bull shit. You know everything there is to know about someone before you even allow them to breach that little bit of an opening you allow others into. You protect this family like you would a newborn child of yours."

"Thatcher is my husband. As of a few days ago, we became parents. No one knows that as yet. With you coming into the family, I wanted to make sure that my son, Jimmy, was safe. I've checked you out, and other than a jaywalking ticket that you had your first day on campus, you've been as clean as whistle." Anna said that she knew that. "What you

11

don't know, or I'm assuming you don't, is that you have a warrant out for your arrest. Your brother Junior has said that you injured him last night. While I know that it's not possible, I'd like for you to tell me why he'd do such a stupid thing."

"Junior is a lazy fuck. If he'd have to look for me for whatever reason he has in his tiny mind, then it would take too much effort. This way he can have me found with little effort from himself, and he can get, what *I'm* assuming, is the money I may or may not have on me. But he'll still take his pound of flesh while he's at it." Rogen said that Anna had turned him in, and that had gotten him in prison this time. "I did. I'm not going to deny that to him or you. He was a jackass, and killed that man as surely as you're breathing."

"The man that he killed. How much do you know about that?" Anna looked away. "I thought so. You were in love with him, Bart Hodges. He killed him over a dispute that you were going to marry him and Junior didn't want that to happen. Why?"

"Because, as sick as this sounds, he wanted me for himself. But I wasn't in love with Bart so much as he was in love with me. He was, I guess you could call him, safe for me." Rogen asked if what Junior wanted was sexual. "No. Just as his domestic. He wanted me under his rule so that I could work, bring home the bacon, cook it for him, then clean up after him. And as wonderful as that might sound, I didn't want to spend my life taking care of my brothers and father."

~*~

Morgan was grading tests when someone knocked on his door. Seeing his father there, he put down his pen and waited for him to yell at him. He hadn't any idea what he'd done, but his father had worn that same look on his face when he was upset about disciplining them as children.

Since Anna had been nearly raped just down the hall from him, he'd been keeping his door open most of the time. Today was the first day that he'd shut it to get some work done. And honestly, he wanted to hide from the world a little. It helped that Professor Long was dead, but he did worry he'd be caught up in something.

"Rogen said that your mate will be released today. Did you know that?" He said that he didn't, that she'd kicked him out three days ago. "Yeah, that's what I'd been told she'd done to you. What are you going to do about her living arrangements?"

"Nothing. Why?" Dad said that he didn't think her being out there alone was a good thing. "Well, I think she's a good deal stronger than you think, and can take care of her brother with one hand tied behind her back. She sure didn't have any trouble taking care of me."

"You let her." Morgan asked him what that had to do with anything. "I don't rightly know. But it's not setting well for me with you just abandoning her."

"I didn't. I have a guard on her at all times. There are as many as five wolf pack members with her every place she goes. The car that has been lent to her in the guise of Rogen letting her use hers has a tracker on it, as well as a panic button. That was Rogen, in the event you thought that I was smart enough to do that." Dad said that he didn't have any doubt that he could do whatever he set his mind to. "Thank you for that. But about Anna. She's pissed off. And me being around her isn't making her any less so."

"What happened between the two of you?" Morgan leaned back in his chair, not even sure what he could say to his dad about all this. "You have no idea, do you, son?"

"No. I mean, I never have rushed her. But she has it in her head that I'm going to take over her life and then make her do things, like her brothers did. Also, I've been, through Rogen, keeping an eye out for her brother that's been released. She's working on trying to figure out what happened at the prison to have gotten him out. Junior's name isn't on any kind of record as having good behavior, nor did he get an early release. But he's on his way here." Dad asked him what he'd want. "Her. And it's not what you're thinking. I thought the same thing. But he wants her to be his house maid. Cooking, cleaning, and anything else that needs to be done. Also, she's to work so that he won't have to. Nice family she has there."

"We've dealt with worse, I'm sorry to say. Rogen, she's got a handle on all them boys too?" Morgan said that she was looking into different areas, that all of them had been in jail until recently, when Junior got out. "That have anything to do with why she's shoving you away?"

"Yes. All of it, as a matter of fact. She has it in her head that she's only a half breed, and not fit for me. Also, she has this insane thing about money, and how she doesn't have any." Dad told him that he could understand that. "I can too. But I don't have to like it. I'm giving her space. For now. As soon as I get information from Rogen, I'm going to go and see her. I'm going to tell her everything that I know."

"Rogen, she told me that you had her do a background check on you." He nodded. "Did you read it?"

"No. It's not something that I can change now anyway. I know that there is nothing serious in it, or I'd have not made it into the position that I'm in now. The reason I gave it to her is because she mentioned that I knew everything about her and she knew nothing of me." Dad asked him what he knew about her. "Not all that much, really. I know that she was working two jobs to put herself through college. She's smart in that too, not overwhelming herself by taking on too many at once. Her grades are great. Anna would have been on the dean's list if not for the fact that she's only taking classes part time. There was only twenty-four dollars in her account until yesterday."

"You think she's going to be upset with you for doing that without asking. I'm assuming that you didn't ask." Morgan just smiled at his dad. "I see. So you're trying your best to make her upset with you, is that it?"

"Pretty much. She is so beautiful when she's mad. I don't tell her that, of course. I don't have a death wish. Besides, in order to ask me about it, she'll have to contact me. And that is going to bring me to her. At least that's my plan." Dad laughed, asking him if he thought that was going to work. "I can hope, can't I? Besides, Dad, she really is going to be in deep trouble if her brother finds out where she is. They think she'll come to heel, I think, and she won't."

"No, it's doubtful that she ever did. Do you suppose she's going to be hurt by them?" Morgan said if they did harm her in any way, they'd never live to tell about it. "No, I don't think they will. And it'd not be just you doing the killing either. Your mom, she sure does like her. Oh, did you hear about having to meet up at Thatcher and Rogen's house tonight for some surprise? Everyone is supposed to show up. I tell you, I hate surprises more than anybody does."

"I do as well. But think of it this way—they might have an announcement to make or something." Dad perked right up. "I have no idea if that's true, Dad. I was making a joke. It

15

probably isn't that at all."

"Well, a man could hope, couldn't he? They have been sort of hiding away in that house of theirs. I ain't seen hide nor hair of them very much over the last week. What do you suppose they're doing?" Morgan said that he didn't have any idea. "Well, I'll see you tonight then. And if you want me to, I'll sweet talk that mate into coming over too. She likes me."

"Everyone likes you, Dad. You're a charmer. And the biggest bullshitter I've ever met." Dad just glared, but didn't deny it. "I have to get to work here if I'm planning on meeting you at Thatcher's house. After I grade these papers I have to find someone to come in and repaint this room. I don't think the sucker has been redone since before I was born."

Dad looked around. "Yeah, I think you might be right on that one. It looks to me like it's been puked on a couple of times too. Is that blood over there in the corner?" Morgan looked and wasn't surprised to see something that did indeed look like blood. "If you want my opinion, I'd take out all these old windows and put in ones that are tighter, as well as something that will keep the wind out. I'd sure hate to come here some morning and find you a Popsicle or something."

"I've put in a request to find out if I can do that. This building is pretty old. I'm betting that they tell me that it'll ruin the way the whole thing looks to have windows put in that are more efficient than the ones that are in the rest of the building." Dad told him that he needed to put in something. "I agree. Tomorrow, while classes are about over for the summer break, I'm going to have my desk brought in here. That way it'll free up some room for me from this monster."

"That desk is older than you are, I'd say. You might want to ask one of your brothers if they want it if you can get rid of it. It's a fine desk, but much too big for this room." Dad looked around. "In fact, son, I'd take out some of these here shelves too. There is no cause for you to have all of them in here when you really don't need them, do you?"

"No. I don't. That's on my list too. I can redecorate anyway that I wish so long as it doesn't harm the structure of the building. I think a bomb could explode in here and it'd not hurt anything within a mile of my office." Morgan jotted down another note on his to do list. "This room is supposed to be an upgrade to the one I had. It is, sort of, but not by much."

The door behind his dad opened and Anna walked in. Morgan stood up and Dad practically ran from the room, closing the door behind him. Morgan could tell without asking that she was spitting mad about something. Whatever she was pissed about, he was sure that he was the one that she was going to take it out on.

Chapter 2

"What the hell were you thinking when you decided that my bank account, with my name on it, needed you to fiddle with it?" He said that she wasn't going to be overdrawn now. "I'm forever overdrawn. It's none of your fucking business."

"It is, actually. I don't want you, no matter how you feel about me, to go without when you need something. The check that you wrote on your books for the summer quarter was going to bounce. The banker, a good friend of mine, understood that we were mates, and knew that I'd want to make sure you were financially secure. He only mentioned it because if that check were to bounce, you'd have four to five more bounce and really put you out of joint." Anna told him that she wasn't at all out of joint. Morgan only looked at her. "All right. I'm pissed off. You have no right to do things like that without telling me about it."

"You wouldn't have allowed me to do it had I asked you first, now would you?" Anna sat down in the chair across from his desk when Morgan spoke again. "What else is upsetting

19

you? I want you to know that I can help you if you need it."

"I don't fucking know what I need anymore." She looked up at him, wondering what sort of money one would have to pay to look as good as he did. "I went to sign up for classes, and was told that all three of them are filled. Then she asked me if I was your mate. Before I could deny it, she moved things around and I got into all of them. That is no way to treat a student who was late filling out the form to take the classes. What did she do, move someone out of it?"

"She more than likely filled out a secondary chair. They do that to make sure that all the classes are filled up for a single class. Why would you deny something — us being mates — that is true?" She didn't answer him again. But he did sit down. "Anna, we have to come to some kind of resolution about us. I know that you don't think you need me in your life, but I have to protect you. Did you hear from Rogen?"

"Yes. This morning. She called me to tell me about Junior. Did she tell you?" He nodded. "He's coming in this direction. Of course, Dad and the other two idiots are in a prison in this area too. He could be going to visit them. But I'm as hopeful for that as I am you not really being my mate."

"That's hurtful."

Anna got up and went to the window, and looked out over the campus while he looked at her. She knew that he was — she could almost feel him touching her with his eyes. "I don't know why I said that to you. It's not true. I've already figured out that having you and your family around is going to not just open doors for me, but close them tightly as well. When Junior gets here, and he will, he won't stop at just trying to tell me what I need to be doing for him. He'll take the years that he's been in prison out on me too."

"I guess that's better than no reason for you to want me to hang around." She turned and looked at him. Really looked. Damn, but he was a really good looking man. And strong too. "I'm sort of uncomfortable about the way you're staring at me. It feels like you're looking for a place to stick a knife."

"I'm a fool." Morgan told her that he doubted that. "I am. I've been running from my family since I was old enough to get out on my own. I've done nothing with my life that could be considered a change. I have no money, no home of my own, and I'm using a car that was supposed to be something that was extra and not being used. Was her telling me that something that the two of you cooked up so that you could keep tabs on me?"

"I don't need that to keep tabs on you even if I wanted to. You're a grown woman that is smart enough to know what needs to be done and how. Rogen, believe it or not, likes you and, like me, wants you safe." He patted his lap. "If you come and sit on my lap, I'll tell you all about the things that I don't know about you. You can ask me whatever you'd like to know about me too. We'll call it a getting to know each other meeting."

"We don't have time for you to be fucking around." He wiggled his brows at her. "You're nuts. Besides, aren't I a little old for you? I mean, I'm pushing thirty."

"I'm almost thirty-four. You know as well as I do that we will both age slower than humans. We'll stay healthier. Also, I don't know if anyone has ever told you this, but you don't even look like you're old enough to drink, much less pushing thirty as you said." She snorted at him. "Are you going to sit on my lap? Both me and my tiger would be much happier if you did."

"You just want to get lucky." Morgan nodded. "You won't be happy with me when my family shows up. Even if it's only Junior, there will be shit that you, as my mate, will have to help me with."

"I would die for you, Anna." She hadn't expected him to say that. It was the first time in her life that anyone had ever said anything as nice as that. "What do you want to know?"

"I don't know, Morgan. I'm so overwhelmed. When I went to sign up for classes, I thought that I'd only take one, which is usually all I can do living the way that I do. But when you said that you had money, it was my plan to piss you off by taking three classes. Then after signing up for them, I realized that was childish. So I paid for them myself. As you well know, I couldn't afford that either."

Finally moving across the small area to where he was sitting, she sat on his lap. Anna was surprised that he didn't grab her or pull her to him. He just let her perch on his leg like she was ready to bounce. That, for some stupid reason, made her angrier than before. Not at him, but at herself again. While not looking at him, she started telling him a story of when she'd been younger.

"I guess I was about ten when I asked for a birthday party of my own. All the kids in my class were having them. No one invited me because I was dirty and my clothing smelled, but I knew about them." He asked her why she would think that was why they didn't invite her. "I knew that my clothes were worn out and dirty. There was barely running water in the house, much less a washer and a dryer. But this birthday party was going to be all mine. The first one that I had. As it turned out, it was the last one too. My brother helped me with the invites. I was old enough to read, but I didn't look over his work. I know that I should have, but I was happy. He wrote dirty words on the cards, telling the people I wanted to invite that I was only inviting them for their gift, to send cash if they couldn't make it. There were curse words on them too. Ones that I'd heard, of course, but didn't have a clue what they might mean. There were things like that. I was humiliated and belittled by not just my classmates, but my teachers as well. It was a nightmare that I never was able to live down."

"What did you do after that?" Anna did lean back on him then. When he only wrapped his arms around her waist, she closed her eyes, thinking about the day after she'd handed out the invitations.

"The teacher read each and every one of them to the entire class. Of course, she bleeped out the words that he'd put on there. The entire time that she was reading them, I had to stand right next to her. Be shamed just a little more." Morgan told her that he was sorry. "So was I. After that, I'd walk down to the laundromat and wash my clothing, and hang it over anything that I could to dry it once a week. Sometimes it was difficult for me to find the money to do it, so I'd run errands for the neighbor. I mowed her grass for her. Then when she paid me, instead of hiding it in the house, I'd have her hold it for me until I could get to the laundry. She liked me being around so much that she allowed me to use her washer and dryer after that. After a while I could buy me things that were hand me downs. I'd worn my brother's underwear that he'd outgrown until then. Then they figured out what I was doing."

"They beat you, didn't they?" She nodded. "Was there more to it than that? I need details so I know just how to deal with him when he shows up. Or, and I like this too, I have to hunt him down like the animal he is."

"They took my money and divided it up among them. There wasn't a great deal by then. Clothing, even second hand, wasn't cheap. After they bought them each a wine or beer, all that my money would net, they tied me to the chair and drank a little and spit it on me. For two whole days it was like that."

"I want you to know that when he does show up here, I'm going to kill him for his treatment of you. Just letting you know that." She kissed him on the chin and Morgan laughed. "What will I get if I take care of all of them for you?"

"You'll just have to wait and see." She allowed him to hold her. "I've never had anything new in my entire life. I don't know why I just thought of that, but I haven't. I've been wearing other people's cast offs for so long, I don't know what I'd do if something had an actual price tag on it."

She was suddenly on her feet and he was pulling her around his desk. Asking him where they were headed got her nothing. It wasn't until they were in his truck, a very nice big truck, that he finally turned to her.

"Did you know that we're expected at Thatcher's house at six?" She nodded at him. "Good. It's about two now and… have you had any lunch yet? I'm starved."

"No, no lunch. Where are we going?" He started the truck and smiled at her as he backed out of his space. "Morgan, what do you think you're doing?"

"We're going to get us a very lovely lunch. After that, we're going to hit the mall for some fancy duds for you. Don't tell me no, because you have no idea how excited I am to do this with you. Will you try them on and come out and model them for me?" She laughed when he wiggled his brows again.

"Oh, and shoes. Sexy high heels so that I can wonder what sort of things you have up under your dress. You will wear a dress for me, won't you?"

"Yes. If you get this excited about shopping, what are you going to do if we have kids and have to take them school shopping?" He pulled the car over, pulled her to him, and kissed her. It was a kiss like nothing she'd ever had before. Claiming. Possessive, and explorative. "Morgan, you keep that up and we'll never make it to your brother's."

Morgan grinned as he pulled out onto the highway again. "As much as I'd like to take you up on that idea, we have to be there. If not, then I was told that I'd be brained. And while I don't think that Thatcher would hurt me — not too much, anyway — I'm positive that Rogen would. Or she'd pay someone to hurt me. She's like that, you know?"

"Yes, I have figured that out as well. You're afraid of her too, then?" Glancing at her, he laughed and said that any sane person would be. "I guess you're right. But I'm sure that she has a soft side. I'm not sure where that might be right now, but I'm betting she has one."

They ended up at a nice little restaurant that served soup and coffee. She wasn't a big fan of either, but they also had nice salads, as well as sandwiches. Anna ordered a salad with chicken and pecans on it. Morgan ordered himself a large sub and chips.

They were seated when he took her hand into hers. Anna was so afraid this was going to be the big brush off or something.

"Whatever is going on in your mind right now, it's not going to happen." Anna asked him what he thought was going on in her head. "I have no idea. But seeing as how you're very negative about such things as being around me, I want you to realize that I'm never going to harm you. I will never make you do anything that you don't want. And here is the biggy. I love you, Anna. With my heart, body, and soul."

She looked away before speaking. "I've fallen in love with you too, but I still think this is a mistake. They're going to come here. Each time one of them is released, they're going to come here to find me." Morgan said for them to come on. "They'll harm you. Not just physically, even though you don't have to worry about that too much. But they will try and hurt you financially, as well as mentally."

"I would hope that I'm a little smarter than them when it comes to mental abuse. But I've never had to deal with that sort of bully, so I don't know for sure." She said that she could understand that because of his family. "Thank you. By the way, my family loves you too. Very much so, and they will protect you with their lives."

"I know that too. It's why for the most part I'm so overwhelmed. They're very touchy-feely too."

Morgan threw back his head and laughed. She had to smile—there was something so endearing about this man when he laughed. And no matter how much she tried to make him pissy with her, he just walked away. Morgan wasn't the least bit violent through words or fists. She thought that was something she loved about him as well.

~*~

Rogen didn't really want anyone to come over tonight. They'd had Jimmy for two weeks now all to their self. Sharing their newborn son seemed like she'd lose some of her ability to hold him when she wanted. Hug him when she needed it more than him. But she knew that they would find out sooner or later, and telling them would cause less problems.

"They'll be here in an hour. Morgan called to say that he wanted to make sure that it was fine that he brought a gift. I asked him what he thought he'd need a gift for, and he cursed. I think he was trying to get an idea as to what we're going to tell them." She smiled at Thatcher. "I'm surprised that no one has figured it out, the way we've been bringing in diapers like we're trying to increase the stock price or something."

"He does use a lot of diapers. But I don't care if we have to spend our last nickel on him. I love this kid that much." Thatcher picked Jimmy up. "When you hold him, he looks about ten times smaller than when I hold him to me."

"Because, my dear wife, I am bigger than you. Thankfully." They sat there together on the couch and said nothing for a few minutes. Then when Jimmy was asleep again, laying across his daddy's chest, she spoke to Thatcher quietly.

"I've found out a great deal of information on our new sister. She's had a hell of a life, Thatcher. It's small wonder that she has a hard time trusting." He asked her what it was that bothered her so much. "The brother that is coming here—and there is no doubt that he is—Anna turned him into the police. He knows it. Also, he wasn't released. I don't even think the prison knew he was missing until I told them. They assumed that he'd been a dead body that needed to be shipped out. Junior slipped himself into a body bag, and when the coroner's office came by to pick up the dead, there were two more that had died that week, he didn't think anything about picking up the extra one. He's on my shit list too."

"So, presuming that he was dead doesn't explain why they didn't miss him before now. What did he do to cover that?" Rogen told him that she was looking into that too. "You think that someone is dirty on the inside, don't you?"

"Yes. I'm sure of it. Junior isn't the first convict to pull this shit. Six months ago, two other 'bodies' were taken out. The coroner isn't really aware of it, I don't think, but I'll get into that after I figure out who the dirty person or persons are." Thatcher said that he had no doubt that she'd figure it out. "Such confidence. I am worried about Anna, however. She claims that she's a half breed, or something along those lines. I have a few questions for you."

"All right. But I might not know the answers, just so you know. Mom and Dad will if I don't, I'm sure of it." Rogen told him that she was asking him first so as not to get them involved just yet. "Why? Is it bad?"

"I think it might be. Is there any way that you can figure out if someone is only partly tiger? I mean, other than a search of her background." He said tasting her blood would work. "Okay, barring that, because I'm not sure she'd let you at this point, is there some other way?"

"I don't know. But I would think that there is." She said that she had an idea. "You don't think that she's a Hayes, do you? Do you suppose they kidnapped her or something? Is that what you're thinking?"

"There are traits that I know only a full blooded shifter can do, correct?" He said there were a great many of them. "I thought so. I've yet to see her tiger—none of us have, for that matter—but I'd bet anything that with her green eyes, she is no more related to the Hayes family than I am. Hayes Senior has brown eyes, and from what I was able to get from the search on her mother, she too had brown eyes. Could be just as she was told, there was a tiger back along the way, but I have my doubts. She has magic."

"What sort of magic?" Rogen told him what she'd figured out. "That is one of the traits of a pure blood. We all age very slowly, and we heal just as fast. Anna doesn't look a day over twenty, if that. Okay, what else? I'm sure you have a couple more."

"I do. The other day, quite by accident, I saw her shift only her hand into a claw. She was in the field behind Morgan's house, and had brambles all around her. She simply pulled them away with her shifted hand. Is that anything that can be done?" He shook his head. "I didn't think so. I can't do it either. I tried. It would be handy when you get all shitty with me. I can, however, bring down a world of hurt on you in other ways."

"I know that. Please don't. I love you." She laid her head on his shoulder and watched Jimmy sleep. "He's a cougar. I wonder what he's going to be like. Probably just like you."

"Thanks." Thatcher just laughed at her. "I'm going to tell you right now; I'm not going to share him with everyone tonight. He's mine, and I'm going to lay claim to him as soon as anyone wants to touch him."

"Are you planning to kill them all? Because that's the only way I can see this even remotely working." Rogen looked up at him. "Mom and Dad will take him from you without asking. My brothers will hold you in a head lock, which now that I think about it, you'd be able to get free from. Why don't you just share him tonight, and we'll work on your tendencies of being extremely violent concerning our kid?"

"He's the first kid I have." Thatcher laughed. "Oh, all right. I'll share, but I'm not going to be nice about it at all. You can take that to the bank."

"No one would expect you to be anything but not nice,

love." Rogen wasn't sure how he meant that, but she let it go. "When I spoke to Morgan earlier today he told me that he and Anna were going shopping. I have no idea why, but he sounded like they were going to go and have a blast. I hate shopping about as much as you do."

"I don't mind shopping online." Her pager went off. "I have to go and work now for a little while. Not long. I have a new program running, and it said it would take ten hours to download. I'm only giving it five hours. If it's not ready by then, then it's not right. I can't have programs running that long to download onto a server when it might be something needed right away."

The office that she had set up in the basement was a gamer's dream. Twelve monitors had been installed so far, along with her own server, as well as so much other gadgetry that she could power the entire state with Internet and not drain on her work at all. But it was hers, her own private system that could take out a person doing bad shit all the way around the world, even if he was surrounded by twenty other people.

The program was finished downloading. According to her computer it had only taken about two hours to work. Giddy, she moved the curser around until she was centered on Junior Hayes. She could see him so well that Rogen could tell that his face was tatted up, he needed a shave, and his fly was unzipped.

Putting the little blue mark on him, all she needed to do was tell it to run and it would give her everything she needed on the man. Not only that, it would give her a flashback — that's what she was calling it — of things that he'd done in the last twenty-four hours. As that information appeared on the other monitor, she moved the camera around that had caught him to figure out just where he was.

The funny thing about having the longitude and latitude of a person's whereabouts was that she still would need a map to figure out where they were. Not with this new program. She had an exact location of not just numbers as to where he was now, but it updated every time he moved, as along with the street address he was closest too. Also—and this was personally what she wanted; it gave her the direction of the next camera to catch him on.

"Mother fuck balls." He was already in Tennessee. At the rate he was going, he could very well be there in about four days. She didn't need that. Not yet. Morgan and Anna had to settle things between them first. If not, then one or both of them could be seriously hurt.

Morgan and Anna just pulled in the drive. They're a bit early. You want to come up here to show off Jimmy? She said to give her ten minutes. Rogen told him that she was working on a location for Junior. *All right. Jimmy just went up to his room for a nap with the nanny, so they'll not know anything. Oh, I'm to tell you to please be nice to Anna. She's very insecure about her clothes. I have no idea what that means.*

I'm sincere. Does this mean that she's dressed in something that is going to make me have to bite my tongue until it bleeds? She did some more work on the computer and realized that Thatcher hadn't answered her. *Thatcher?*

Honey, you are going to be blown away by the way she looks. It's amazing what fitting clothing can do for a woman. Now she had to go up, but paused long enough to print off some of the pictures so that she could look at them to see where Junior had been, Rogen picked them up and took them with her.

31

Christ, she's beautiful.

As the picture spit out of the computer, two of them caught her eye. Going back to that camera to see if she could make better sense of what she was seeing, Rogen pulled out a thumb drive and saved the picture. Junior was going to get his ass killed, hopefully before he made it to where his sister was.

Even though they were only human, she was sure that they could still harm Anna; if—and Rogen always thought about the "if" of something—they could get past any of them. She hoped they couldn't, but you couldn't tell with idiots. Nor could she dispel the fact that they were Anna's relatives— people that she'd grown up with, anyway.

Going up the stairs, she saw Anna. Christ, she was gorgeous. The dress was a honey yellow. It made her porcelain skin look so much softer, lighter even. While not washing her out at all, it made her cheeks glow, her eyes sparkle in a way that made it appear as if she had a touch of wildness about her that only few would ever know. The slit up the side made her legs look longer, thus punctuating the fact that she was tall. Even in her yellow sparkling heels, she only reached to Morgan's shoulder. Beautiful did not cover how she looked at this moment.

Rogen could hear Anna talking and realized that she was on the phone. Whoever had called here for her would soon know that their asses were Rogen's if they threatened a hair on Anna's head. Rogen would tear them up, and not necessarily with her cat.

Chapter 3

Morgan didn't know what to do with himself. He could feel the anger and the fear surrounding Anna while she was on the phone. But since she wasn't speaking at the moment, he didn't know how to comfort her with this.

Should he take the phone from her? He thought that would get his ass kicked. Could he lean in and listen in on the conversation? No, he was sure that if she wanted him to hear it, she would have offered.

As soon as Rogen came up from downstairs, she handed him a stack of what he thought was about ten snapshots. The top one, he assumed, was of Junior standing over a dead woman with a knife in his hand.

Then she did something that he'd not been able to convince himself to do. Rogen took the phone from Anna. It didn't go to her without a fight, though. Finally, surprisingly to him, Anna won the battle. Rogen told her to talk to him, then showed her the picture that he'd looked at.

"You killed someone? Christ, Junior, what the hell are

you doing? As much as I'd love to see you back in prison, killing someone isn't good. You'll be there as soon as they find you if I have anything to say about it."

Rogen reached over and pushed a button that put Anna's brother on speaker phone.

"What are you going to do, Anna? Turn me in again? That only worked for you the one time—I want you to remember that shit. I'm not going back to prison for you or anyone else." Anna asked him about the women he'd killed. "I don't know how you figured that out about me killing those women, but you can bet your ass whatever I do to you is gonna be much worster."

"What the hell do you think is going to be worse, not worster, than killing me, you moron? Christ, you should have been smothered as a kid. And you'd better have all your worldly possessions taken care of, Junior. If not, then I guess I'll have to deal with them." He asked her what she was talking about. "Coming here. You think you're going to just be able to do what you did to me as a kid? I got news for you now, buster. Once I'm able to sniff you out—and I will, most certainly—I'm going to make sure you never bother anyone again."

"Did you just threaten me, Anna? And if you call me Junior again, I swear to you I'm going to carve my name into your head so that you don't ever forget it. I'm Noah, you fucking bitch. Say it with me." Thatcher laughed when she called him Junior once again. "You got someone listening in on us? Mother fucker, you gots no rights to do shit unless I allow it. I'm going to enjoy taking you apart, Anna. Just you wait and see."

"You might have let this slip your mind at some point

of you getting ass fucked, dumbass, but I'm a tiger. You are not. I'm not anywhere as afraid as you should be." He said that a bullet would take care of her. "Do you really think so? Well, come on then, you come here and try to put a bullet in me, and we'll see who walks away. And Junior, you should be watching your back too. I'm turning you in for murder as soon as I hang up on you."

The phone slammed down hard against the cradle. When Morgan started to reach for her, Anna put her hand over her mouth and Rogen told her where the bathroom was. Morgan watched his mate run down the hall. *Christ*, he thought, *she is as bad as Rogen*. He started to go to her when Rogen put her hand on his chest.

"Wait. There are a couple of things I need to tell you first. Her too, but I think right now, she'll be better taking it from you." He told Rogen that he wasn't so sure of that. "Trust me, it will be better. This isn't the first woman that he's killed. There are three counting this one. All the same MO. He rapes them until they're nearly dead, then he slits their throats. Anna knows how he does it too."

"Where is he?" Rogen told him. "I see. And being that close, I'm sure you have someone on him every step of the way now."

"I have since he was out, but now I have my own set of eyes on him. Junior won't be able to kill again, not if I can help it." Morgan thanked her. "You have to bond with her, Morgan. She'll be stronger than she is right now. We all know that. The time for getting her used to us is up. He'll kill her, or try to, if she is taken by him. With you and her bonded, you know what she'll be after that."

"Yes. Not only stronger, but she'll also have whatever

little bit of magic I got when I was able to shift." Rogen nodded. "Anything else you need from us? I mean, you know I'll do anything to keep her safe."

"Just make sure that she has enough strength and guts to take the fucker on. Also, you might not like this, but she will need to know what is said when he's killed, if it comes to that. If not, then I'm afraid she'll have to live with the unknown." Morgan asked her what she meant. "If she thinks he might have had some second thoughts about his life. He might. It has happened before, you know."

"Do you think he will? I mean, honestly, do you think for a moment he sounded like a man who had a change of heart?" She shook her head. "Okay then. I understand what you're saying. She'll need to be the one that orders his death, or even does it herself, so that there are no what ifs later on. I can't promise you anything except that I'll try to not kill him for her. But if he touches her with intent to harm her, all promises are off."

"You bet your sweet ass they are." Rogen looked at her mate and smiled at him when he stood in the doorway looking all mean and pissy. When he spoke again, she could almost feel his anger toward Junior. "My parents and brothers all just pulled up. Show time."

"What the hell do you have going on?"

She simply walked away from Morgan when he asked. She could hear him laughing, so Rogen made her way to Anna. The other woman was coming out of the bathroom when she stepped into the hall. She asked her if she was all right.

"I'm not sure." Rogen told her that she could understand that. "I don't know that you can. I just signed my death warrant concerning my brother." Without thought as to what

Anna would do to her, Rogen smacked her in the face. "What the fuck was that for? You do know that I can take you on, don't you?"

"I'm sure you can. And I have to be honest with you, Anna. I'm thinking that you could beat my ass about half the time too. I'd rather not put that to the test, but I'm betting that you have almost as much training as I do in the protecting yourself kind of precautions." Anna only nodded. "There are some things I feel you need to talk about with Morgan."

"You need for us to bond." Rogen wasn't impressed by many people, but she was with Anna. Not only did that impress her, but she had a feeling that Anna could beat the shit out of her more times than not.

Anna had grown up on the streets. So had Rogen, but not like Anna had. For Anna it had been fight for her every meal or die. The same with her home life. While Rogen could beat her in a combat setting with weaponry, Anna could beat her with her smarts. How to fight dirty. And there was no doubt that she would, too.

Hearing the front door open, Rogen asked her if she'd hang around after the others left. She wanted to show her a few things. After Anna agreed, Rogen wrapped her arm around her waist and gave her a handgun, without a thought to what might happen when she did so.

Rogen was surprised once again by Anna, who not only checked the magazine for the handgun being hot, but stuck it in the back of her pants as Rogen would have done. This was a woman she thought she could work with, if she'd agree.

While his family was in the living room, Rogen noticed that Thatcher was missing. She knew where he was, and told them all to have a seat, that they had something that they wanted to share with them.

Thatch snorted. "I know you ain't breeding. Whatever else you have to tell us isn't going to be any kind of *good* surprise. I don't know about the rest of these here people, but I surely could use some news like that." She glared at him. It was that or squeeze him in a hug for being just like she'd hoped he'd be. "Well, we all came over here, and that son of mine just took off like he wasn't going to visit with us none. Also, there had better be a dinner coming. I'm about starved. I was too nervous to think about food when we was ordered to come here."

"If I had ordered you anywhere, you old shit, I would have sent armed guards after your skinny ass. And there is dinner involved. But I'm not sure you'll want to eat it when it's ready." He asked her why not. "Because I'm going to maim you in a way that you can't eat. Why are you so cantankerous all the time?"

"Probably the same reason you're a mean girl all the time. What is this supposed surprise?" Meggie told him to behave. "I don't want to behave. I want this done so that I can get on with what I was doing before."

"You weren't doing a darn thing but taking your afternoon nap. After you'd had your lunch nap. Rogen is right, you have become cantankerous lately. Why is that?" He told her what he wanted. "I'm sorry, I don't think I hear you right. You want a what?"

"A grandbaby. And don't you go acting like you don't want one too. Darn it, Meggie, they been married for a month. Surely in that time a grandbaby might well have been—" He looked at Rogen when a sound from the hall caught his attention. "You're not nice, making a noise like that when I just told you that I wanted a grandbaby."

"I didn't do anything, you old poop. Your wife has it about right in calling you that, as far as I'm concerned. I can and might just change your name to Poop Robinson." Thatcher put Jimmy in his mother's arms. Rogen watched as she began to peel some of the blankets off her burden. "Meggie, I'd like for you to be the first family member to meet James Robinson, mine and Thatcher's son."

No one moved as Jimmy, tired of being held so stiffly, screamed his head off. She knew what that meant too. When they'd brought him home they'd tried their best to wrap him into one of those swaddle things, and he pitched a fit. Now they rarely covered him at all.

"Oh my goodness, Thatch! It's a little boy. Our grandson! Look at him. He's perfect." Meggie had him down to his diaper and onesie. Thatch reached over and barely touched his finger to his little toes. "He's beautiful. Is this what you were talking about as a surprise? If not, I can't think of a single thing in the world that would be better than this."

"There is actually one more thing. We've been asked to adopt another child. But since Morgan has found his mate, I wanted to see if it was something that Anna wanted to do this time around. The little girl at the hospital was abandoned legally, and is a tiger, as we all are." If she'd not been looking right at Anna when she spoke about the little baby needing a home, she might have missed the look of hope on her face. It was dashed almost in the same blink of an eye when total disappointment laid there. "She'll be as safe as Jimmy will be. This I can promise you. No one will get past all of us to either baby."

"We love each other, Anna. And while I want to do

this with you with all my heart, I want you to answer the question. She'll be both of our responsibilities. I wouldn't put all the pressure of raising a child on you anymore than I think you would do to me. I promise you that. But I won't put you into a position without you agreeing to this. It'll be a big responsibility for us both." Anna looked at her when Morgan did. Rogen was sure what his next question would be. "What do you know about her? I'm sure you know more than the hospital does."

"I do. Her parents are both deceased. Accident. Great grandparents thought that they could raise her on their own, but as you can imagine, it's a little too much for them. They're both in their mid-seventies. Her name, if you'd like to keep it that, is Marie Renee Broadway. She's six months old and just beginning to crawl. Grandparents are out of the picture too, as they wanted nothing to do with the union because they didn't care for the male mate." Morgan asked about him. "Good person, from what I could tell. Held down a good job until he was killed. They were on their second honeymoon, ten year anniversary. The mother was an attorney. There is a substantial insurance policy that is hers when she turns twenty-one. Not a single skeleton in their closet that I could find. And you know me well enough to know that I looked hard."

"We'll take her."

After Anna agreed to adopt the child, Thatch whooped it up so loudly that he woke up Jimmy. While Meggie was trying to comfort her grandson, Thatch was still whooping it up. "Another grandbaby, Meggie. Did you hear that? Two of them in one day. I'm a man having the next best day of my life."

"And what do you consider your first, Thatch Robinson?" He told her that it was marrying her. "What about these boys here?"

"Oh, love, because they're a part of you, they are right up there at the top of the list with you." He winked at her, and the boys that he called his sons laughed. "I love you, Meggie dear."

~*~

Noah pushed his way through the mall with his cart rolling behind him quickly. They would be closing in about ten minutes, and he had to find himself a place to hide before they did. He'd spent the night in several malls before he'd gone to prison, so he knew this was a sure bet for getting himself a nice place to sleep. The place that sold furniture and bedding was his target.

"Can I help you?" The security guard startled him. "I asked if I could help you, Mr. Hayes. We're closing in about five minutes, and I'm afraid that I'm not going to allow you to stay here in the mall."

It occurred to him that the man knew his name. How that was possible was bothering him enough to want to hit the man until he put his hand on his gun. Mall security guards didn't wear real guns, his mind thought. Just as he was going to jump the man, knowing that he'd not harm him overly much, the guard grinned at him.

"I'm not a guard of this mall, Mr. Hayes. If you're thinking that I am, then you're going to be dead before you reach for me." Noah just stared at the man. That was twice that he'd called him by name. "Now, I think it's time you left."

"How the hell did you find out my name? I'm surely not on any list or shit. I've not ever been in this here mall before."

The man said nothing. His badge proclaimed him as Stafford. "Officer Stafford, is it? Well, I'm not sure where you got your information, but I was here to get me some...some sheets. Why did you think that I was going to sleep here?"

"Because I have people that are a good deal smarter than you are watching out for people like you. Your sister, she was very accommodating in letting my boss know that you've done this sort of thing before. Including going so far as to trash up the place before the doors opened up. Ring a bell with you?" Noah asked him how he knew his sister. "We have a mutual friend, as a matter of fact. I was told by my boss that when I see you, I am to run you off. If that fails, which I'm hoping you do try and get around me, I'm to blow your fucking head off. There would be no one questioning me on whether it was justified or not either."

Noah looked around. He noticed that they'd drawn quite a crowd of onlookers now. He wasn't going to panic — that wasn't his style. Panicking people were stupid people, and Noah thought that he was as smart as any dumbass cop. Noah wanted to inch his way into the store and get lost in one of the changing rooms, but another cop, with his hand on his gun too, came up behind him, blocking his way from getting more than a foot into the store.

"Now, you're going to take your little cart and get out of the mall before I have you arrested or shot. I don't care how you float with this, but either way, you'll not be sleeping in this or any other store in this mall." Noah asked again how he knew his sister. "I don't. Not at all. But she has a friend, as I said to you, that can pull some mighty strong strings, and that got me after your ass. Are you going to leave on your own or in a hearse? As I said, either way is good with me."

"I have never been treated so terribly in all my life. And I just got out of prison." He looked around for someone to come to his aide. He could tell right away that he was on his own this time. "This is tailgating, I hope you know that. Once I'm out of here, I'm calling my lawyer."

"You go right on ahead and tell them you're caught tailgating. I'm sure that will go over well with them. But you might get more action from your supposed attorney if you tell him or her that you've been targeted. Which won't work either, because that's not the way I'm doing this. I was sent your picture to watch out for. I was informed that you're a black spot on society, as well as a thief. In this case, it's sleeping in the mall and using the bed you had no intentions of purchasing." Stafford laughed again. "I was told that if you didn't believe this information came from your sister, then I'm to tell you that you hate being called Junior. Do you, Junior? Do you hate being called Junior?"

"You mother fucker." He nearly jumped at the man's throat, but the guns being pulled on him, both in front and behind, had him take note that he'd never survive this if he did. "Where is she? Where is my sister, Anna?"

"Home, I would guess. With her husband. Also, I've heard that they're going to have themselves a little girl soon."

That was news to him. Anna had gotten married? And had a brat? Noah told him that he lied. Pulling out his phone, Stafford showed him a picture of not just his sister, but a man standing next to her. And Christ almighty, he was a big fucking man. The second picture showed just Anna giving him the finger.

"She sure has a real hatred of you. I'd say that you must have done something stupid—or stupider, in this case—to have made her upset enough to tell me to kill you even if you blinked the wrong way. I'm not going to do that, of course. But I guess now that I think on it, I can understand her being pissy with you. You have two minutes, Mr. Hayes, to get out of the mall, and never return or I'll arrest you for trespassing."

"I'll have you know that I'm going to sue your ass when I contact someone. I might even take a hit out on you for this shit." Stafford asked him if he was threatening him. "No, I'm making you a fucking promise. You just—"

He didn't even get to finish the rest of his promise to the cop before he was snatched up by his legs and dragged right out of the building. All he could think about was wrapping his hands around Anna's throat and smashing the life out of her and that brat of hers.

As soon as he was outside, he realized that instead of it getting cooler out, as he'd thought it would, it was hotter. Not only that, but the humidity was so thick that he was soaking wet all over his face and neck before he could manage to get up off the sidewalk, where he'd been tossed.

Noah had always been a sweaty person. If for any reason he'd be outside just checking out the yard, he'd be sopping wet, from his forehead to the back of his knees. Noah would be wiping that shit off him every ten seconds. That was why everyone thought he was lazy. He was, but mostly, he hated the feeling of sweat all over him. Of course, the great thing about it was that when he was back inside, the air conditioner, when they had one, would cool him right off. Even a fan would do the trick.

Finding other means of getting in out of the heat was proving to be harder than he thought it should have been. There weren't no empty buildings around that he could easily break into. Noah noticed that a lot of empties were being boarded up, like they didn't want anyone coming in to get themselves a nice place to sleep. He wondered aloud what this world was coming to.

Noah finally found him a dumpster that had just been emptied out, and made him a cleaned up place in it. This was what he did in a pinch, and was now glad that he'd not mentioned to anyone what he did. It smelled bad, but he was sure that he did too, so it was all right for the night.

Pulling out his big notebook he'd gotten in prison, Noah added what he'd done today. One of the docs that had worked with him told him that it would help improve his mind if he were to keep a list of things that he had to do daily. Somehow that had gotten screwed up in his head to him writing down things that he had done, not things that he needed to get done. It had been an entire month, a habit by then, before someone told him he'd been wrong.

"Well, he sure ain't gonna be telling me shit like that again, will he?" Noah's soft laughter rang around the metal box he was in. "He's not gonna be telling nobody what they did was wrong without himself a tongue. Ain't that right?"

When the rain started to pelt him like it was pissed off at him for some reason, he had to close up the lid. Not only did the closing of the box make it hotter than hell in the thing, but it also made it stink worster. He thought about his sister correcting him on that when she'd been living at home with them all. Kept telling him that weren't no word.

"Daddy uses it. So does David and Bud. There ain't no way that it's not a word when most people use it." She said no one used it but them, so that wasn't a good comeback. Then she just moved away from him before he could show her what it felt like to correct him and insult the rest of them.

Most of the time he never understood a word that came out of her mouth. Anna would correct them when they were trying to tell her something. He wondered if she did that on purpose, just to get them all addled up about something.

You'd get out about two words, then she'd tell you that you said it wrong. Or used it wrong. It'd nearly take all day for you to get a just sentence out with the way she worked a body. She was like a starved dog with a piece of meat. Anna would keep picking at you all the time, until you just wanted to slap the shit out of her. Which really, he didn't need an excuse to do, but it sure made him feel better when he had one.

Curling up in a ball, Noah tried to get himself some sleep. It was hard. After a bitty bit, he had to open the lid up because of the stinky smell, as well as the heat making him feel like he was on this side of Hell. Getting out proved harder than it had been before prison, and he pushed that off as they were making the dumpsters taller.

"I surely ain't getting too old for this shit." He had to think a minute on how old he was. He had to figure it three times before he settled that there was something wrong with his cow-u-lations. "There ain't no way that I'm pushing forty-nine. No way in hell."

The more he thought about it, the less he believed it at all. If he was forty-nine like he thought, then that would make his daddy nearing seventy. David would be forty-seven, and then old Bud would be hitting forty-five. They couldn't be into their forties like this.

Trying not to think about how old he was, he centered more on how much time he'd lost by being in prison. Long enough to know that he'd missed out on the best years of his life. Prison had taken away his youth, he told himself. What a cock sucking deal.

Making himself another note, he was going to find him a phone and call up either his daddy or one of his brothers. Surely they'd know how old they were without him having to figure it out all wrong. Yes, sir. That was what he was gonna do. Find him a phone and call up his family. The only thing that Noah knew for sure was that he'd been away in prison when he'd first heard about momma having herself a little girl.

"Why in God's good graces would she want to get knocked up with a girl?" He supposed nobody might have told her about having a kid when she was too old to poop one out. "They're all dummies. I should have been there to help her get rid of the thing. I'm sure that's what's wrong with Anna. She's touched in the head."

When he thought that the dumpster was cooled off a mite, he climbed back in. Falling in on his head surely did hurt, but he didn't care. Now he had himself a nice place to sleep. Of course, his cardboard was wet, but that might well cool him off a little too. Lying down, Noah thought of the shit he was going to have to do tomorrow.

Chapter 4

Morgan had never held a baby before that he could remember. If he had, he was sure that it hadn't been as terrifying as it felt right now. Christ, the ones in the nursery that they'd seen were the tiniest things he'd ever seen. He asked Anna if she wanted to hold it first.

"If you don't stop calling her an it, I'm going to make it so you can't hold her ever again. Her name is Marie. Say it. Marie." He grinned at her and said her name. "Dammit, what is taking them so long to get here?"

"They're making sure that she's fit to be taken home. Checking all her nooks and crannies to make sure they're giving us a healthy baby." Anna glared at him, telling him that she was a baby, how many nooks and crannies could she have. "I don't know, love. But I do know that you're going to be a great mother."

"I hope so. I just wish now that I'd thought this through a little more before agreeing to it. What if something happens and I drop her or something?" Morgan told her that she was a cat. "I suppose, in your insane logic, you're telling me that you think she'll land on her feet. What a stupid thing to say. No wonder you didn't date much."

"Who told you that?" She said his mother had. "My mother, as much as she likes to think she knows about me, doesn't know shit about my dating life. I could almost forgive her for that, but I'm sure she told you, too, that I went to my junior and senior prom without a date. It was because I couldn't ask all the women I knew to go with me."

"Oh sure, that's what happened." Before he could tickle her, something that he'd only just found out she hated, a nurse came in with a small crib in front of her. "I thought you forgot about us."

"Good gracious no. We have been so busy down here today. I think that we've had twelve deliveries. These little girls are just doll babies." Morgan heard what she said, but apparently Anna hadn't. "Here you go. Aren't they just the cutest little things you've ever laid eyes—?"

"There are two of them? I thought.... We were told that there was a little girl and her name was Marie Renee." The nurse nodded at Anna. "Then are you showing us the wrong children? I'm confused."

"No. I don't know what happened about that. But this little one is Renee, and her sister—identical twins, by the way—is Marie." Anna was handed Renee and he took Marie. "I bet I know what happened. You just wait here a minute and I'll find out for sure."

This time she did return in a minute. Mary was armed with not just a bottle apiece for the babies, but also diapers and wipes to change them with after, she told them. After making sure that the babies were getting their bottles, she explained what had happened.

"We had this new girl working the desk. I said had, because she only lasted about a day. You'd not believe the mess ups that she made in such a short order of time. Anyway, I bet that's what she did. Told you their names by mixing up that they were twins. The man that came in earlier for a set of twin boys, he was sure fired up about not getting two for the price of one. His words, not mine. I'm kind of glad that he didn't take him." Mary looked at the two of them with a look of disappointment on her face. "You're not going to take them now, are you? I'm so sorry to have wasted your time on this. I could just brain that girl for—"

"We'll take all three of them." Anna looked at him like he was nuts. He probably was. Morgan was sure that he'd regret this as soon as he had to feed all three of them at once. "If we don't take them, someone like *two for the price of one* guy will take them, and there is no way I'd be able to sleep at night wondering what he was doing to them."

"Mr. Morgan, it would be a handful for any parent to take on three children at once. Are you sure you want to do this without knowing a thing about children?" Morgan nodded. The more he thought about it, the more he was keen on the idea. "You don't have to do that. You know that, don't you?"

"I do. You know my parents. You know that once they figure out that we have three more children for them to play with, they'll never leave our home. I can see them now. They'll be lined up on the front porch with Jimmy in their arms to kidnap them all for the night."

Anna nodded at him. "They're waiting at Thatcher's home now to see the little girl that we were going to bring back with us." Anna smiled, and he would take on a thousand babies to see her looking that happy all the time. "Trust me when I tell you, we'll have so much help that we'll be lucky to see them at all once we take them from here. Morgan is right. We'll take all three of them."

When Mary walked away, Anna fed Renee. As she spoke to the baby about the things they were going to have to get themselves before they could even leave here today, Morgan sat down as well. Feeding his daughter her bottle was great. He didn't think that he messed up very much either.

"I'm going to call the closest dealership to here and order us a bigger car. Also, we'll need to get three car seats instead of just the one. I'm sort of glad that Rogen lent us hers so we could bring her home. You know that she would only have the best, and that is what I want for our children." Anna said that she was glad that she'd taken a picture of it so they could order while in here. "I'll see if someone will bring us those. I doubt they'll say no. This is going to be something I bet they run into all the time."

"We don't even have them a bed yet." Morgan said that for one night, they could sleep between them. "Sure, like I'll be able to close my eyes with the three of them between us. Oh, and diapers. I'm thinking after what Rogen said about how many times a day she has to change Jimmy, we'll need to have them delivered by semi. Just have one backed up to the side door of the house and unload them as we need them."

Anna was finished feeding Renee when Mary came back with another little crib. The little boy was tiny. Much smaller than his older sisters were. He asked her about that.

"He's a newborn. The girls are a little older than him, but he'll catch up to them and surpass them soon enough. If you can think of a name for him—no pressure—I can get his birth certificate filled out for you. Also, you should know that the woman who had him abandoned him at birth. Since she left him here when she was discharged, she can no longer lay claim to him." Anna said that was going to be her next question. "Now, you know the girls are tigers, correct? Well, the young man here is wholly human. But that doesn't even worry me. You two would be wonderful parents to even a snake should it need a helping hand."

Morgan made four phone calls. He called for a large SUV to be brought to the hospital, and then made two calls to two different children's stores to get car seats delivered to the hospital and baby beds delivered to their home. Since they knew exactly what they wanted, it was easy for the stores to get them to them. The last call he made was to Shane, the pack master.

"I'm a man in desperate need of help." Shane laughed, asking him what he could do for him. "Don't tell anyone yet, but Anna and I hit the jackpot. We're coming home with three babies."

"Sure you are." Morgan told him that it was true several times before he could make him believe him. After explaining to him what he needed, Shane said he'd get into the house after Morgan gave him the code to get in. "Setting up three baby beds won't be that hard. It's you that has a hard life coming to you. Over the next month, you're going to be begging me to take them into my pack."

"No, I don't think I will on this one." Shane said he was joking. "I'm not. Christ, Shane, I just met them, and I'm already in love with them. How anyone could just walk away from this little guy and these little girls…. I don't understand it."

"I don't either, my friend. My daughters are all I have left in this world, and as much as I loved them the day that they were born, it's immeasurable how much I love them now."

Morgan looked at his wife and son as he took his bottle while his sisters were snoozing in the crib. After hanging up with Shane, knowing that everything would be done before too long, he sat down with Anna. He needed to know if she'd marry him now. Not just because of her brother, but he was going to put her name down on the birth certificates as his wife, if she'd allow him to.

"We need to be married for real now." He nodded at her, wondering if they were forever going to be thinking alike. "If you've changed your mind, now is the time to tell me."

"I haven't. I want to be your husband more than anything." She looked down at the baby in her arms, and so did he. "He's going to need someone to protect him more than the girls will. Being human to a houseful of cats might make him jealous too. I don't ever want him to feel that way."

"I was jealous of my brothers for being human. Of course, that was before I figured out that I was ten times stronger than any of them." Morgan laughed with her, and the baby opened his eyes and stared at her. "He's beautiful, isn't he? I mean, look at those beautiful green eyes."

"They're a beautiful as yours are." Anna asked him about a name. "I'm assuming that you don't wish to name him after your side of the family. Correct?"

"No, not in any way, shape, or form." Morgan thought of his great grandda. "Do you have someone that you admire? I have just a couple of people, but they're your family as well."

"I was just thinking about my great grandda. He was a spicy old man. And I say it that way because we weren't allowed to call him Buzzard. Grandda could curse better than you and Rogen, fish like it was his job, and never put out his hand unless it had something in it. A small piece of candy. Sometimes it would be a quarter or less. He loved us all so very much. He would have been head over heels in love with you, and Rogen too." Anna asked him what his name was. "He was Edmund Bauer Robinson. My dad's grandda."

"That's a wonderfully strong name. What did everyone call him? To his face, I mean." Morgan had to think about it, but just couldn't remember. He'd only called him Grandda. "How do you feel about Eddie? It's short for Edmund, don't you think?"

"I love that. My dad, he'll know better than me what he went by, but I love Eddie."

When Mary came back with a list of things they were taking home with them, he got a call from Shane telling him that the beds were set up, and that his daughters had put sheets and the rest of the things on the bed. "What other things? We only ordered the beds and sheets."

Shane was laughing when he disconnected the call. Just as they were packing things in the bags that the hospital was giving them, he was notified that his car was there and that the car seats had been put in the back seats. He was so happy for that.

"Thatcher told me that he could take out a person's heart, repair it, and put it back with more ease than it had been to put the car seats in the car. We'll need to get another car for you, as well as seats for that one. I don't ever want to have to take them out now that they're in there." They were laughing when Morgan heard from his dad.

You ever coming back here? Good heavens, man, I want to see my granddaughter. Morgan told him that they'd need another two hours for paperwork. *I don't like it, but I can understand, I guess. You just make sure that you bring me that little girl home. Your mom is not letting me hold Jimmy like I want to.*

I'm sorry about that, Dad, but like you said, we need to get the paperwork finished up before we can come back. I tell you what, why don't you meet us at our house? All of you. I know that Anna is worn out. She's still getting over being hurt, you know. Dad said that was a mighty fine idea. Anna smacked him in the chest and winked at him. *Thanks so much. I know that Anna will appreciate it too. She can take a nap if she wants.* This time she punched him in the chin. It wasn't hurtful; in fact, he found it to be funny.

Well, we did go ahead and eat. None of us were going to last much longer waiting on you two. I guess you're three now, aren't you? Morgan didn't say anything as he watched his son being put in one of the car seats. *All right. We'll finish cleaning up here, then we'll get on over to your house. Poor Anna. She's gonna need us to move in there with you to make sure she doesn't overdo it. Don't you think?*

To that, he had no comment. But he was glad for the extra time. It would take them only about fifteen minutes to get home, and then they'd be ready for when his family showed up. They were going to shit a brick.

~*~

Anna watched the children as they slept. The staff that had been here when she moved in were as excited as she and Morgan were about the new additions. After parking the car in the garage so as not to give anything away, Morgan came into the house. She was glad to see him when the girls woke up.

"Mary said to let them lie on the floor on a blanket. They'll need tummy time. I'm terrified that we'll step on one of them." Morgan said that he wouldn't dare, and Anna laughed. "Do you really think this was a good idea? I mean, it's really too late now—I've fallen in love with them. But there are three of them, and only us two."

"My dad said that he and Mom need to move in with us to help you out with just the one baby." She hit him again. "You know you're very violent, aren't you? I'd just let them play on the floor. If they're still there when my family comes over, it'll be fun to watch them find them."

Anna put Renee on the floor while Morgan did the same for Marie. Almost as soon as they were down, they made their way to each other. They weren't really crawling so much as dragging their body around. Once Marie got up on her knees, she looked as if she'd completed the best thing in her little life. She was laughing as she rocked herself back and forth. Not really moving yet, but Anna had no doubt that she'd be going soon.

The knock at the front door had Morgan rushing to it. Anna sat down on the couch, trying her best not to be nervous about what his family would say about the children. Thatch asked her how she was feeling.

"Fine. How are you?" He looked at the bassinet in the room. "I guess we're all a little tired after the day we've had."

As he was moving toward Eddie, Renee came around the side of the couch where she was sitting. Meggie found her there. Her picking Renee up had Thatch turning, and he did not look like a happy man.

"Darn it, woman, I was going to hold her." Morgan went to the bassinet and handed him Eddie. "What's this? You got a boy and a girl while you were there? Or is this one here on loan?"

"I don't think they loan children out, Dad. But no, we didn't get us a boy and girl while we were there." It was Thatcher that found Marie, and his face was a perfect picture of confusion. Morgan was laughing while he explained. "The girl wasn't a girl at all, but twin sisters. Meet Renee in Mom's arms. Thatcher has Marie. The little boy you're holding, Dad, is Edmund Bauer. We'll be calling him Eddie for short."

Thatch stared at his son for several long seconds. Anna was ready to take Eddie from him, fearing that he hated both the name and the child, when he grabbed Morgan around the neck and pulled him to him. The hug tugged at so many heart strings that she had to look away for a moment to gather herself.

"You named him after my grandda." Anna nodded at him when he looked at her. "Two granddaughters and two grandsons. I don't think I could take much more. There's not another one lurking around, is there? I don't think I'd be able to take it, son. I just don't."

"Just the three of them."

Jimmy was laid on the floor with the girls. They didn't touch him, but they certainly gave him the once over. Thatch just sat in the chair next to them and held Eddie in his arms. Anna told them what they'd found out when they went to pick up their one daughter. Or so they thought. "The little boy was left there by his mother. When she was released, she said that she didn't want him. The woman at the desk had messed up that the girls were twins. The man who was to take Eddie decided that he didn't want just a single child. Instead of leaving him behind, we decided that he'd be just as happy with us. I think he'll be fine."

"He's a handsome little man, I'll give him that. Him and Jimmy are going to be best buds, see if they're not. All of them about the same age, it's gonna be tough raising them without any help." Morgan told his mom that they were going to hire pack to help them out, but that they'd be very hands on parents. "Of course you will be. You're all going to be wonderful parents."

Morgan's brothers each held the children. She got the biggest kick out of Dawson. He was trying to make sure they were all right without anyone noticing. They might not have if he didn't pull out his stethoscope and listen to each of their hearts.

"They did all that at the hospital, Dawson." He laughed and said that you can never be too careful. Morgan laughed as he continued. "I guess not. But we do have to take Eddie in for his next test the day after tomorrow."

"I can do it, if you'd like. That way he can have his mommy hold him when I have to stick him." Morgan looked at her and she nodded. "Good. Have you picked a pediatrician yet?"

"We have a list of things that each of them need. Neither Renee nor Marie have had any troubles, of course. They're both up to date. But Eddie was slightly jaundiced when he was born, so we have to have him checked a couple more times to make sure that he doesn't have anything wrong with his liver." Beckett asked her if they were going to dress them all three alike. "I never gave it any thought, as a matter of fact. Even though we've only had them for a few hours, I can already tell the girls apart. They have very distinct personalities. Marie is more adventurous, while Renee likes to watch and see what is going on before she makes her move.

Also, Marie is greedier than her sister, and will suck down her bottle quickly. Renee will take hers, then look around a minute before she gets back to it. So no, I don't think I'll dress them the same. Not unless it's for a special occasion anyway."

"Here's something that I noticed about Marie that you probably already know — she's not happy with being held for too long." Anna told Meggie that she'd noticed that as well. "Yes, I thought you might. There will be no cuddling this one unless she needs it. And even then, I think she'll hold out."

Meggie got up with Marie and sat down next to Anna. "You think that I'll do all right with these three?" Meggie asked her why she didn't think she would. "I don't know. I don't have a lot of good role models to gather from. I was hoping that you'd not be too upset with me if I did screw up."

"The only way you can screw up with a child is not to love it at all, or giving them too much. They'll know that you love them. I know that it's not the way of the world right now, but if they need their bottoms spanked, you do that too. Giving them no discipline is as bad as not loving them." Anna told her that she'd never beat them. "Well, of course you won't. I never thought that you would. No, honey. I think that between you and Rogen raising your little ones, they'll be ready for the world. And know how to protect themselves better than most, I would imagine."

Meggie put Renee on the floor, and she started her move toward her daddy. It was funny to her to think that in the short amount of time that they'd had them, they had attached themselves to Morgan right away.

"When we first went to get what we thought was going to be one child, I had this vision of Morgan holding his son while a little girl scrambled up his leg to get him to hold her

60

too. There was already one on his shoulders. I didn't know at the time that we were going to have just that vision. Those little girls, they already love him so very much." Meggie told her that they loved her as well. "I'm sure they do. I'm not being whiney about this. I know that Morgan has a lot more confidence in himself than I do in me."

"You'll soon enough realize that not only are you stronger than you think you are, but that you have an inner strength in you that all of us can see and are waiting for you to find." Anna asked her what the strength might be. "That your love for these children and for my boy surpasses every imaginable magic ever made or used. That, my dear child, will keep you and him very safe."

"They all think we should bond soon. I do as well, but they seem to think it will make my cat stronger." Meggie said that it would. "In what way? I wasn't raised by cats, so I'm not sure of a lot of things. The only reason I was able to shift was because I was pissed off at one of my brothers, and anger brought her out."

"I don't really think you're related to those monsters anyway. Do you?" Anna had been thinking the same thing for the last couple of days. Mostly how she really didn't look like any of them, not even her mother. "If you are, that's fine as well. They made you who you are today, and we can be thankful for that. The same with Rogen and her parents. Her dad and mom drove nearly all the way across the United States to talk to her, to tell her and Jamie that they were sorry for what lousy parents they both were. Not that I think your family is going to have a change of heart about you, but one can hope."

"How would I go about figuring this out? I mean, if

61

I'm actually related to them or not." Anna watched Beckett down on the floor with the girls, trying to teach them how to crawl. They were doing a much better job than he was. "I'll do whatever it takes."

When Meggie didn't answer her, she turned to look at her. Meggie was staring at something. Turning to look, she saw the man's face in the window of the door to the outside. Standing up, she asked if anyone knew the person.

"No, but you can bet that I'll find out who he is." Rogen moved to the door. Before she could open it, Morgan said he'd get it. "Why? Because you're the big man?"

"No. Because if you get hurt, even a broken nail, while dealing with this man, I'll never forgive myself. If I need you, I swear, I'll be the first person to scream help. All right?" It was funny the way Rogen agreed, like she was still pissed off but realized he was going to be all right. "Thank you. I know how much that cost you to allow me to open my own door, Rogen."

"Just open the fucking door before we won't have to, because you'll be hanging through it while I deal with the intruder. Doesn't he know that you have a front door, for Christ's sake?" Morgan said he'd make sure he knew that for next time. Anna burst out laughing. "What are you laughing at? He might be here to kill you or something."

"I think that he wouldn't have allowed us to see him, then waved at us." When Rogen pouted, Anna revised her statement. "But then, I could be wrong. Next time you can break down the door when someone comes around."

"I hate you all. I just want to put that out there."

Morgan was laughing when he opened the door. Almost as soon as it was wide enough for them to be seen by the man, he started talking.

"You stole my son. I have called the police, and you'll be going to prison for kidnapping." Morgan asked him what he was talking about. "The kid at the hospital. You took him when you wasn't supposed to. I was gonna get two, but they screwed up. I want that kid back now."

Then he did just what Rogen had predicted. The man pulled out a gun and pointed it at the room in general. Anna didn't move except to reach down and pick up one of the girls. Meggie had the other. She could only hope that Thatch had Eddie still, and he was safe as well.

Chapter 5

The police were snickering so much that Morgan wanted to go and knock their heads upside of something hard. It was sort of funny, but the way they kept looking at Rogen he thought for sure they were going to piss her off enough that she would do as she threatened and pull in the big guys. While he knew what that meant, he was positive that these cops didn't. Otherwise they'd be shutting their trap pretty fast.

"Morgan, did you ever see the man before today?" Looking back at Andy, he told him no, never. "You said that he came here looking for a boy, one of your children? Why did he want your son?"

Morgan told him again what had happened at the hospital. "We adopted the three children. The staff there thought that he was a little off because of some things that he'd said when there was only the one male child. Anna and I, we felt like it was something we had to do, not just because of the man, but just one of those sort of creepy feelings you get. You know, like someone stepped on your grave, as our parents used to tell us when we were kids." Andy nodded and said that his mother still said that to him. "There was a mess up when we were called about the children. When Anna and I showed up, we thought that we were going to come home with one daughter. But they were twins. I can only assume that his call was messed up as well, and he thought that he was getting twin boys. Two for the price of one, he told the nurse, I think she told me."

"Yes, that's what she told us too." Morgan wanted to ask him why he was still questioning him when he knew the story as well as he did now. Turning when he stiffened, he nearly burst out laughing when Rogen had one of the officers down on the ground with a knife at his throat. But what he found more funny was Anna standing over another officer with her hand shifted to her cat and holding him at his chest. The vest, he knew, would not survive the claws of a large cat, at least a large pissed off female cat. "Ladies, please don't hurt them too much. It's hard enough getting people to work for me."

Never missing a beat, Andy started talking to him again. When they finished up, he then stood where his men were and cleared his throat. Whatever he had to say, Morgan thought that he'd better tread carefully around the women.

"Did I not tell you before we pulled up to keep your mouths shut? I even warned you about wiping your feet on the rug outside the house." Neither man spoke. "Rogen, could you please allow him to breathe? I think that he's turning a nice shade of blue. Anyway, you were even warned, several times, not to piss these ladies off, weren't you? Blink if you understand now the importance of not pissing them off."

Both men blinked so many times they looked like they

were those blinking lights on a Christmas tree. Shaking his head, Andy walked away. But before leaving when the coroner did with Mr. Paterson, Andy turned to him and Thatcher.

"Do you suppose that when the other women show up, you could give me a heads up on how they are? It would do my crew a lot of good. Although, I was thinking that tangling with one of them would certainly put them on their toes, don't you think?" Dad was now talking to the men while he jiggled Renee on his shoulder, who was asleep. "You know what, guys? I don't envy you at all with these women. I know for a fact that I'd be scared shitless every day on what I said to them. You guys must have bigger balls than me. Mate or not, I'd be running in the other direction. But they sure are easy on the eyes, aren't they?"

"They are at that, Andy." Thatcher patted him on the back. "What happens now with this thing with Paterson? Had it not been for Anna protecting her kittens, I have no idea what might have happened here."

"I agree with you there, Thatcher. I have no idea what might have been going through his head when he'd been told not to touch her children. Christ almighty, I wish I could have seen it. The coroner told me that he messed his pants before he died." Andy looked at the broken back doors before turning back to them. "Nothing can be done about a man having a heart attack, is the way I'm seeing it. Of course, most people would be terrified out of their minds when a little bitty woman like Anna there was suddenly a big Bengal tiger."

"Thanks, Andy. Anna really was protecting them. She must have told him six times to leave the house, and that you guys had been called. Then when he grabbed little Jimmy's leg hard enough to have him screaming? Well, I think Rogen will be pissed off about Anna beating her to the draw on that." Andy told Morgan that either one of them would scare him. "Some days they do me as well. But I love them both with all my heart."

After Andy left with his men, Dad got out a broom and started cleaning up the mess. He wanted to hold the babies again, but he said that he was a little too shook up right now. Dad had both Jimmy and Eddie in his arms when the man touched the boy. Morgan also thought that his dad was a little embarrassed about what had nearly happened.

"You all right, Dad?" He nodded, then shook his head. "That man, he didn't hurt any of them. You know that, don't you?"

"I just froze up, Morgan." He looked around and then stepped out onto the lawn after laying the broom down. Morgan followed him. "I was so afraid of him doing just what he did. Then when he had the balls to reach out and grab that little boy, I just stood there like an old fool and about let him."

"No you didn't, Dad. I saw you holding onto him like your life depended on it. He would have gotten him, too, had you not jerked back out of Anna's way when she came at the man." Dad told him that he'd messed up, and nobody would let him watch the kids. "Are you kidding me? We're all so grateful to have you watching over them that Thatcher and I were just talking about how we'll be able to take out our wives when we want a break."

Thatcher came through the door, and must have heard what he'd said to him. "I thought that you'd left, Dad. Rogen needs a night out. I don't suppose you and Mom will keep an eye on Jimmy, will you?" Dad eyed him hard. "Dad, I swear to you. I was just coming out to ask Morgan where you'd gone. It would be all right if you can't. It's been a rough day for all of us, I think."

"You told him, didn't you?" Morgan said that he'd not said a word. "You did this because you think this old man is feeling sorry for himself and needs this. Well, I don't need your—"

"What the fuck are you screaming about?" Both he and Thatcher backed away from Rogen when she came out. "Did he ask you to watch the kid for me, Thatch? Did he tell you why we need a night out? For the next four days I have to run maneuvers for the navy. Nothing bad, but I won't be able to leave the house. I just got the call."

Rogen looked at Dad, then at Morgan. She looked confused. If she was in on this little plan of his, he was never going to play any card games with her. Rogen was scary good at keeping her face neutral.

"You feeling sorry for this old man too?" Rogen asked Dad if he thought that she had a single sensitive bone in her body. "That man, he nearly took your little boy. Did you see how I just allowed him to do that? I'm not worth spit when it comes to those—"

The slap to Dad's face startled both him and Thatcher. Both of them, already a good two feet from their dad, took another few steps back. Dad glared at Rogen for a minute, then burst into sobbing tears.

"You almost lost that son of yours because of me." Rogen asked him if he wanted her to hit him again. "No. You proved your point. But you have to be worried about me and what might happen."

"There are a lot of people that I worry about, you old poop, and you aren't even in the spectrum of being anywhere on that list. That man did not get my son, nor any of the other children that were there playing on the floor, because you were smart enough to have them in your hands. What do you think would have happened had they still been on the floor? He would have taken them out the door before any of us could have attacked. Also, you got the four of them out of harm's way when Anna beat me in knocking the shit out of him. Christ, Thatch, as far as I'm concerned you're a hero. I just can't think of anything else to say to you but thank you." Dad said that he was sorry anyway. "Listen, you know me well enough to know that I won't lie to you. You also know that I would tell you if you fucked up. Right?" Dad nodded. "You didn't do a dammed thing wrong. If you had, I'd be wiping up that blood and glass with your ass. Now, are you going to watch Jimmy or not? I don't have time to fuck around with you when you're being stupid."

He said he'd watch him for her. When Rogen walked back into the house, telling everyone within ear shot that she was going out to dinner tonight, Dad looked at him and Thatcher.

"I don't want you to tell her that I said this, but I'd warn your kids' teachers about her coming to meetings with them. She might well have the entire armed forces coming in to see what crap they're doing to her kids." Dad shook his head. "I tell you, boys, if the next mate that comes here is anything like those first two, I might have to see a doctor about getting myself some nerve pills. I don't think I can take another one like them."

"Sure you can, Dad. You know as well as the rest of us that you have both those women wrapped tightly around your finger." He said he'd thought so too, but wasn't so sure now. "Nah, they love you very much. Also, I think you learned a valuable lesson tonight too, didn't you?"

"Yes I did. Do not, under any circumstances, try and be emotional around either one of them." Dad rubbed his cheek. "She sure has a wallop on her. Do you think that Anna will too? I'm not going to test the waters on that one. I've learned my lesson."

After Dad left, Morgan looked at his older brother. He asked him if he'd heard him talking to Dad. Thatcher said that Anna had, and sent Rogen to talk to him.

"I'm excited about the date, don't get me wrong. But the way those women plot, it sort of makes me think that if they were in charge of the country, things might be a little better off." Both of them laughed as they started cleaning up in the living room again. "Also, I don't know if you realize this or not, but there is no way that Anna is a half-breed tiger."

"Why do you say that?" Thatcher knew more than most about such things as being pure blood or otherwise. "Did Rogen tell you that she wants Anna's blood to be tested by you to make sure?"

"She was able to shift, then change back in less time than it took me to realize that she was on the attack. Not to mention, did you notice that she was dressed after shifting?" Morgan hadn't, but did remember it now. "I can do that. I'm sure that you can too now, with a mate. But Rogen can't. She's not a pureblood. You and I both are, and have mates. Dad told me that was what happened when we found out mates."

Shane came over just as Thatcher and Rogen were leaving, and helped them board up the doorway so that nothing could come in during the night. Tomorrow Morgan would call someone to fix it for them.

Picking up Anna when everyone left, he sat on the couch

and held Eddie and Renee while she finished feeding Marie. He was just dozing off when Anna told him it was time for bed.

Christ, what a day. He'd become a father of three, and had a broken door because someone had tried to kidnap one of them. Anna loved him, and his dad had been slapped by Rogen. Morgan was happy to see the end of this day. He was exhausted.

~*~

Anna woke and realize that she was alone in the big bed. This was the first night that she'd gone to sleep in his bed, and they'd both been so tired that they'd fallen asleep almost as soon as the lights were out. Getting up, she ran to the room next to theirs to check on the babies.

Morgan was asleep on the floor as his big cat, with all three of them around him. Going back to get her cell phone, she took several shots of him with the kids, and then joined him on the floor. He woke up just as Eddie started fussing.

I got you, little man. Morgan winked at her. *I just couldn't stand the fact that they were all alone in here. The girls haven't stirred at all, but he's being a little fussy tonight. Mom told me he might be with all these people holding him.*

Anna picked up Eddie, then stood up to change him. "It might be because he's soaking wet." She was getting pretty good at changing his diaper, she thought. She'd only had to refer to the picture on the box once this time. "I have a doctor's appointment tomorrow with your brother. He wants to have them tested for their lineage. I had no idea that was even a thing."

"It is when a child is left like the girls were. It's not invasive, but it will tell us a great deal about their family tree and such." She asked him why that might be important. "Well, for one thing, if they're a child of a leader, they'll have strength that isn't common in just shifter tigers. They might even have a few traits, such as fur color, that might not be like the rest of the tigers. There are different colored tigers like there are people."

"I never thought of that." He nodded as he told her that there were also long lines of tigers, at the beginning, that were inbred for different reasons. "That I can understand as being an issue. I'm glad that he's doing it. He should more than likely test me as well while he's at it, I think."

Taking a bottle from the little box next to the changing table, she measured out what she would need to make Eddie a bottle before putting him into his bed. Morgan was back to his other self and putting Renee and Marie into their beds. He just stood over them, watching them.

"The mobiles that the pack gave us are beautiful. Did you notice them?" Morgan said that he had, and had forgotten to thank Shane for them. "Thank them for the blankets too. Did you see that each of them have one on their beds? They'll be wonderful for this winter. And I bet that they're handmade, too."

"Yes, I agree." Turning to watch her feed Eddie, he smiled at her. "We've really screwed things up between you and me." She asked him what he meant. "Well, we have three children, a house, are supposedly married, and we've never even had sex."

"Would you like to?" Morgan nodded. "I would as well. I thought about jumping your bones tonight, but as soon as my head hit the pillow, I was out like a light. Now we have three little ones that need our attention all the time. I feel like

I overdid it—if you understand that."

"I do, and when I heard Eddie fussing a little while ago—I didn't think to check his diaper—I was suddenly overwhelmed with it all. Three little ones in diapers, learning to crawl, then to walk. It's a lot, even if we weren't insane, like I believe we have to be." Anna laughed, then burped Eddie. The sound that came from him sounded like he'd been holding it in for a while. "Well, that might explain a lot. Sheesh, that had to come from his toes."

After putting him to bed, they stood over the cribs and watched the three of them sleep. "We'll need help. I don't mean for just an occasional night out, but all the time. While I want to believe that we can do this on our own, I'm reasonably sure that we can't."

"I was thinking the same thing while in here on the floor with them. I can already see that they have different ideas about how they like to sleep. Mom said that she noticed it as well. I'll ask Shane about it tomorrow." Morgan turned her to him and wrapped his arms around her. Anna looked up at him. "I want you. So very much. But I have to tell you, I'm worn out."

They both laughed. "Will it be like this all the time, you think?" He said that he hoped not. It would crush him. "Yes, me too. How about we go to bed and see just how tired we really are?" This time it was her that wiggled her brows. "You, my fine sir, have a very needy wife on your hands."

"Good. I think I can do something about that." Kissing the children again, Morgan picked her up in his arms. "I don't want you completely worn out. This way I can conserve a bit of your energy for later."

Instead of putting her on the bed like she thought that he

would, he stood her in front of him and began to undress her. All she had on, really, was a pair of panties, as well as an old shirt of his. He asked her if she liked her new clothing.

"I do. I especially love the shorts that I got. The ones that make a little of my butt show? I won't wear them in public, but I will show them to you here in the privacy of our home." He kissed her, stealing her breath away as well as making her heart beat faster. "You make me wild when you kiss me like that."

"You make me want to be an animal with you when I see you like this." She stood before him in only her panties. They weren't much covering for her, and she was sure that they were wet now.

Shifting on her feet, she saw his nostrils flare. Anna leaned into his throat and inhaled his scent into her body. There was so much that she wanted to say to him, to do to him as well, but her body wasn't responding to anything but him. To what he was doing to her.

When he turned her around, Morgan massaged her breasts, his cock at her backside. Every new place he touched her, it was like he was waking her nerve endings. Bringing to life, for the first time, all of her senses.

Turning around so that she faced him, Anna almost begged him to not touch her right now. To let her rest. But then he dropped before her, his hands on her hips. All she could think of in that second was that she was going to wake the babies with her scream as soon as she came.

His mouth left her weak in her knees as he devoured her. His hands made her back and ass feel like he was putting electrical currents through her body. When he suckled on her clit, all she could do was bite down hard on her fist as she came screaming behind it. It was that or shout her head off.

There was no rest for her now. Morgan managed to bring her several more times before she begged him to let her sit, to let her do something other than to sway on her feet. Anna should have known that he'd have a plan for her this way. Almost as soon as she sat on the side of the bed, Morgan pulled her to the edge and continued to feast on the most tender part of her body.

Lying back on the bed, she pulled a pillow over her face. Anna could let go now, not hold back on the noises that she wanted—no, desperately needed to make. When she came again, her scream seemed to echo around her head until she simply passed out.

She must have only been out for several seconds. When she woke, Anna found herself in the middle of the bed, her head laying on pillows that were cool behind her neck. As Morgan moved up her legs while he sat at the bottom of the bed, she watched him, keeping an eye on him so that he'd not do something that would have her passing out again.

"You enjoyed that, I think." She nodded, her throat raw from her releases. "Now it's my turn. My turn to make you feel like I do every day when I see you. With every breath I take, I can smell you nearby. I need to feel you become as much a part of me as I can make you. I love you, Anna Robinson."

Morgan didn't just slide into her, but he seemed to possess her. The weight of his legs on her, the way his arms seemed to keep her from exploding, was like a lifeline to her. Just as she lifted her legs up, wrapping them around his waist, she felt him take her hard. It was like he was really going to become one with her. And Anna couldn't wait.

It was a pounding that she loved. Her body responded to

his administration as if it had never had sex before. Taking in as much as she could of him, Anna begged him to come. To fill her with his body so that they'd forever be one.

His tiger raced over his skin, and hers did the same. Her nails extended out of her fingertips as she clawed him down his back. When Morgan threw back his head, his body bowed back in a profile that made her body scream out her release. Then he did the most incredible thing — he roared out.

She'd only ever heard a male do that when she'd visited a zoo. It was so much more erotic than she'd remembered it to be, the way his own claws tore into the mattress, holding her there so that he could fill her over and over until he was emptied of himself.

Morgan dropped on her, his body spent, his breath coming out in short pants. Every inch of her felt as if it had been abused, but in a beautifully eye opening way. When he nudged her chin up, his mouth at her shoulder, she closed her eyes to the final part of their coming together.

As soon as his teeth sank deeply into her flesh, Anna came again and again as he suckled at her wound until she lost her vision and passed out once again. Even knowing as much as she did about mates coming together, it shook her world until she was sure that the house would no longer be the same.

Anna had to crawl out from under him when the sun was blasting into the room hours later. She could hear the girls jabbering. Eddie was awake when she entered the room, but he'd not gotten awake enough to let them know that he was ready for his breakfast. Changing him first, she put him on the floor while she handled the girls.

Since they were older, they moved around a great deal more than he did, which was fine. But her body was worn out, and every new strain on her muscles made her wince. As soon as Morgan joined her, talking to Eddie about him being a good boy, she carried Renee while Morgan brought down Marie and Eddie for their breakfast.

Anna wasn't sure she could give this experience up to someone. While she was still tired, she loved the smell of their fresh skin. The way that the girls seemed to be having a conversation with them. They would need help, she knew, but for today, she was going to enjoy this for as long as she could. Anna loved being a wife and mother. It was the best thing that had ever happened to her.

Morgan was talking to the children as he fed them their food. "Today we have a big day, guys. Not only do we have to take you to see Uncle Dawson, we're going to get Mommy a new car, some more car seats to carry you buggers around in, as well as something other than T-shirts to wear." They were jabbering right along with him. "Then after that is finished up, we're going to see about getting a nice nanny or two to help out with you, so that Mommy and Daddy can have some fun without you. Then dinner at my parents' house."

Anna smiled at Morgan. His brother was right—Morgan was going to be a great dad to these guys. And she was going to do her best to be a great mom too.

Chapter 6

Noah waited for his dad to be brought out to talk to him. He had thought for sure that he'd have a bit of difficulty getting in this place, but they'd just waved him through and had him sign off on the paperwork. He knew what it said. It wasn't that long ago that he'd had the same paperwork shoved in front of him. Then he saw his father.

He had aged a great deal, Noah thought. Not only had he lost a great deal of weight that he really needed to shed anyway, but he also had cut off all his hair so that he was as bald as a bowling ball. As soon as he sat down and picked up the phone, he asked him who he was.

"Your son. Noah Junior. Don't you remember me?" Dad nodded, then looked away. Noah thought that he was being spoken to from the screws on the other side that he couldn't see, but waited. He didn't want to lose this opportunity to tell him what he'd done. "Dad, I'm out."

"No fucking shit? Here I was thinking that you were one of them hallow grounds or something. Why don't you start with saying something smart? You know, something that I want to hear. Dumbass." Well, his dad's way with words hadn't changed at all, Noah thought. "What you doing out, anyhows? I thought that you were in for a couple of lifers, or close to it. Got yourself some religion or something that makes it so you've been behaving? I won't believe that even if it is true."

"It's not true. I was just smarter than the system. I was going to talk to you about Anna. She's married, did you hear that?" He put his hand to his ear like one would so that you'd know they were listening. "I guess not, huh?"

"You're dumber than cat shit, you know that, Junior?" He nearly told him that he didn't go by Junior anymore, but even through the glass he was sure that his dad could hurt him. "Now tell me why you'd think that I was awaiting to hear about that dumb fuck daughter of mine to marry off. She's more than likely knocked up too, I'm betting. Marry someone without shit too. If they think that I'm going to be picking up the tab on them raising dumbass kids like the three of you were, then you can forget that. I'll stay right where I am forever."

"She married a man with money. She was trying to better herself by going to college. At least that's what I heard through the grapevine." That statement was one of the dumbest ones he'd ever heard. Who talked at a grapevine anyways? Dad told him that women didn't need to be educated. Men had enough trouble with them when they tried to hide their pussy from them. "I guess you're right. About the kids. Nah, she's not knocked up. But she has a kid now. Something about adopting them or some shit. If she's got that kinda money, she can hand some of it over to me, I'm thinking."

"Don't." He asked him what he meant. "Don't think. You ain't bright enough to let your head do the talking for you. Not even when you're talking like you are to me. Sometimes I wonder what the hell your momma was thinking giving me three of the dumbest kids on this here earth."

"That's what I came here for. About Momma. Was she a cat like Anna is?" Dad said that she wasn't. "Yeah, I didn't think you'd care for that. The reason that I'm wondering is because the people where she's living now are all tigers. Even the rich people. Got themselves a whole town of freaks like them. How do you supposed that Anna got to be one and we didn't?"

"She ain't mine and your momma's kid. Never was." That surprised him. He'd always thought that Anna was their baby sister. "One other time when I was in here, your momma had a friend of hers that died in some kind of plane accident. I don't know much about that on account'a I was in here, but your momma decided that she'd help this friend of hers raise up her baby. I tell you, Junior, I near beat her to death after I heard about that. Didn't even know she was not human until it was too late to take her out back and drown the little bitch."

"Is that why Momma died?" Dad looked around, then nodded at him. "I guess you don't have any idea who the parents are either, do you? That would help. Maybe I can find them to sell her back to them."

"Didn't I just tell you that she was dead or something, moron? Christ almighty, dumbass, get the shit out of your ears and listen to what I'm telling you. You know how much I hate to repeat myself."

Yes, his father did hate to repeat himself. Noah had a couple of more questions, but he had to run them through his noodle before he could ask them. He didn't want no repeat of getting his head bashed in like his father did to him as a kid.

"You know that I didn't kill your momma, don't you? Yeah, I did beat her around a good deal. It was fun, and she was good at keeping her mouth shut after that." Noah started to protest that he'd just told him that he had killed her when he spoke again. "She was always good for a few punches to the face when I was pissed off. But her bringing that fucking cat to my home would set me off no matter how poorly she was feeling. It was all her fault for thinking that she could have a single fucking thought that I'd approve of. So that last time when I was showing her who the boss was, she didn't come around anymore. Her head was too badly hurt, they told me."

"Why didn't you take it out on Anna? I'd think that's what I'd do." His dad just stared at him with a wrinkled up forehead. "Well, it sure would have fixed it so that she wasn't around no more."

"You just don't think no more, you fool. Did you just hear what you said? Take her on? Did you not remember that she's a big fucking tiger? One that has big teeth and claws? Why the hell would I try and take that shit on when your momma was so much easier to tame?" Dad shook his head at him. "Me take on a damned big cat when it could have gotten me killed. Is that what you want? For her to have killed me off?"

Dad stood up and was told to sit down. It was loud enough and firm enough that his dad did just that. But he was pissed off. Noah was glad now that there was a thick glass between them. He'd have surely hit him if there weren't.

When he was calm again, Noah asked him if he needed anything. Of course, that set him off again. He wanted out, damn it. There weren't no reason for him to be locked up when there were bigger and meaner criminals around.

Dad was taken away after that. Noah was sort of glad for it. Dad wouldn't listen to him now even if it was the best plan in the world. As he sat there, his brother David came to sit in the chair. They had told him at the desk up front that David might not be allowed to come out.

"I got me a girlfriend." Noah asked him if there were women in this place. "No, dummy, she's outside awaiting on me."

"For what? Are you planning on getting out?" David said that he was going to as soon as they made him take a test. "What sort of test are you taking, David? One to show if you're still a dummy?"

The plastic between them shattered when David hit it. Noah had forgotten how much he hated to be called a dummy. Or any other word that made him sound like he was stupid. But dummy, that was the worsterst one ever.

As the guards tackled his brother to the floor, Noah stood back out of the way. There was blood on the plastic, he could see, and the thing was just a little bitty punch away from being gone. Noah shivered when he thought of the damage that David could do to him in a little bit of time.

It took nine men to hold him down until he was handcuffed to the floor. Then another two to hold him still enough to give him a shot to knock him out. Noah didn't envy the person that had to lift him up and carry him back to his cell. David was well over seven feet tall and weighed about four hundred and fifty pounds. Most of it was muscle too. David liked to work out.

Going out of the building, he wasn't stopped. Noah

thought for sure they'd be pissed off because he'd riled up his brother. His dad too, he supposed, but not nearly like he had David. Actually, he thought it was funny that he had. Walking to the car that he'd stolen, Noah wiped the leaves off the front windshield and got in. The air was up to full blast when he left the parking lot.

He'd been picking up rides since he'd made his way to Ohio. Noah had learned that trick when he'd been arrested a while back. His roomy had told him about it. Keeping them guessing, that's what he was doing. If the police were looking for you in one car, you'd be in another one before they put out the bulletin on your ass. It was easy poesy, or however that saying went.

Now all he had to do was to find Anna—not his sister. That blew him away to have found that out. Noah had gone to see his daddy about another matter. He needed to know if he was getting out soon. If so, then he'd wait on getting the cash. All the robbery money from when he'd robbed the bank before being caught, it was there for the taking. But Noah knew his dad would kill him for taking it if he got out soon.

"Mother fucker probably used it all up, is what happened to it." His dad had done that before. David had gone with him to rob a store. Beings that his brother was so big, instead of killing anyone with a gun, he'd had David crunch in their noodle. Little did any of them know that it was still a felony to have David doing that shit. He was a lethal weapon. "Who would have figured that the big dummy was a weapon?"

Laughing at his joke, he found his way into the little town that he'd been able to trace his sister to. No, not his sister, but a woman that was a cat. Noah knew something about the rules that were used for being a cat or any other shifter. She couldn't hurt her own kin. It was forbidden or something like that. It wasn't just a rule, he'd been told, but they couldn't do it no matter what. It was in their UPS or something.

The town that she was living in was nothing more than a wide spot in the road. There were a few nice houses, but not nearly as many houses as trailers that lined up like a choo choo train along the river. How anyone could live in one of them suckers was beyond him. The floor would fall through when you was doing your business. Then there was wind troubles. They'd fall off the shit they'd be sitting on and you'd be homeless again.

Pulling up in front of one of them ice cream places that also served a good sammich, he waited in line at the window with the rest of the people. They was mostly kids, he supposed, from the high school, but he didn't mind. There were plenty of pretty girls to make him happy.

"Did you hear about Mr. Morgan? He and his new wife have three kids now. I sure hated to see him off the market. Man, what a good looking guy." The girls around the one talking agreed with her. "But Anna is really nice. She's looking for a nanny to help out with the kids. And she's looking for sitters for when they want to go out, too. His brother, Mr. Thatcher, paid really well when I sat for him a couple of weeks ago."

"What's Anna's last name?" They all turned to look at him like he was a dirty bug or something. "I'm looking for my sister, and her name is Anna. That's all I want to do is find her."

"If she's your sister, then don't you think you'd know her last name?" Talker was going to get her face punched if she got smart with him again. Noah would be thrilled to pickles to do it to her too. "I don't know you from Adam. I'm not telling you shit."

"My name is Noah, not Adam." She stared at him for a moment before she and her little twitters started laughing. "I asked you a question, and you'd better give me a name before I bust you in the chops, girly."

"Danielle, Sara, you guys go on now and leave this jerk to me." He turned around and started to hit the woman behind him when he realized that it was his Anna. "What the fuck are you doing bothering kids, Junior? Don't you have better things to do than fuck with my day?"

"I should just knock you on your fucking ass for what you've put me through. My name ain't Junior no more. It's Noah." She asked him what he thought that she'd done to him. "You had me arrested, you cunt. Why would you do that to...? Well, I started to say to your own brother, but we're not related at all. Did you know that?"

"Yes." He didn't know what to say after that. While he was thinking up another question, she spoke again. "My parents are both dead. It was a plane accident that took their lives, as well as those of a few other people. Your mother, Ruth, took me in when she was asked to watch over me while they went on this two day trip. Your father wouldn't have ever found out, because he was doing ten years at the federal prison, so she did it. When the plane went down, Ruth decided that she'd keep me as her own."

"I knew that." She said that he didn't. "Yes I did. Dad just told me all about it. I knew it a long time ago."

"You just found out that he told you this a long time ago? As usual, Junior, you're as stupid as they come." Before he could draw back his fist far enough to hit her, she smiled at him. "You hit me, even to brush a little wind around my face, and I will tear you apart. I'm not joking either, you moron. I'm a tiger, while you're nothing but a pile of shit on a warm day. You should also know that I could have had you arrested the moment that you made your way out of prison in a body bag, but I wanted you to come here."

"Why? You gonna ask me for my forgiveness? I ain't gonna give it to you. You will be hurting much before I'm done with you." Anna said that she had no reason to ask him for shit. "What if I decided to come on into your house and make a mess of them little babies?"

"You'll never get by the front gate. Trust me when I tell you, Junior, you are as good as dead as you stand here. I just want to see what sort of shit you can get yourself into before the Feds come down on your ass." He asked her why they'd be doing that. "Murder. Robbery. Then there are the stolen cars, all nine of them. By the way, you left your prints all over each and every one of them. Did you ever hear of gloves?"

"They was too hot. And you lie." She only stepped up to the ice cream window and ordered four sammiches, as well as fries and drinks. "I'm not going to eat with you, bitch."

"No kidding. This is for my husband and me. We're taking the kids that you were talking about out on a walk. It's a lovely day for it, don't you think?" Noah wanted to hit her and take all her food. "You have fun now."

Noah was also starving. When he'd left the prison behind, he could only think of one thing—a creamy chicken sammich. Those, as far as he was concerned, were a national treasure chest. Damn, but they were good. And when Anna picked up her food, there were four of them suckers right there on the tray, with the biggest order of fries that he'd ever done seen.

His belly made sure he knew that he was wanting one too.

Walking up to the window, he ordered himself three of them to eat all by himself. "I'm sorry, sir. Mrs. Robinson just took the last ones. I could make you a hamburger if you'd like."

He wanted the fucking chicken sammich, damn it. He made his way to Anna to demand that she share hers with him.

~*~

Morgan stood up when Junior approached them. He was impressed that he had the balls to do that, come up on Anna knowing that she was a cat. Morgan had a feeling that he had no idea that he was one as well, and a pissed off cat as well. Anna just continued to feed the girls little bits of her sandwich as she ignored Junior.

"You will give me one of those sammiches right now. I've come here just to get me one of them." Morgan simply told him no. "No? Do you have any idea who I am?"

"Junior Hayes. Not that it means a hell of a lot to me, but that's who you are." Junior said his name was Noah. "Not to me you're not. Why don't you go away and leave my family alone? Or better yet, why don't you just walk in front of a truck or bus and be gone from our lives forever? That would thrill a great many people to death, I think."

"You're a big man, talking to me as if I'm nothing at all." Morgan simply let enough of his cat go so that the man couldn't help but see him. "A fucking tiger? You're one of them there shifting things too? Holee Christ buttons. Am I the only normal person in the fucking world?"

"Normal? I doubt anyone would think of you as normal. You're insane if you think that we're going to put up with your shit now that we know who you are." Morgan watched his face set into thinking. It was as if he was using every bit of his body to work out whatever was going on in his head. "Don't hurt yourself. Just ask me."

"How did she know that she wasn't my sister when I didn't even know? A man should know these things." Morgan asked him why he wanted to know. "You done told me to ask you, didn't you? Damn it, you can't be changing the rules right in the middle of me asking."

"My brother Dawson has come up with a program that can tell what a person's lineage is. It's for shifters that cannot use a human company to find out where they might be from. Once he found out that there wasn't any way that Anna was born of your family, Rogen, my sister, looked to see how many tigers were born around your area. She found out that the Markell's lived right next door to you up until their death in a plane crash. It took a little longer to figure out that they'd had a child. A child that they left in keeping with your mother when they went away on a trip. When the plane went down, your mom figured that no one would notice that she had a daughter that she hadn't birthed. I think, up until your father murdered her, your mother was quite happy having a child around that didn't beat on her or steal from her. I would have been, I believe." Junior said that he'd not murdered her, she died later. "She was murdered by all of you—if only I were able to take you all to court over it. You used your poor mother as a punching back until she could no longer get better between beatings."

"No, you got it all wrong. I just now talked at my daddy. He said that Momma brought that cat, Anna, to the house and he'd not approved of it. She died because she wasn't healing right in the head. That had nothing to do with her dying. Sure, we all knocked her around, but she liked it. Momma learned her lesson right quick when we told her to shut up and she didn't." Morgan wasn't the least bit surprised that this moron would think that his mom deserved what she got. "Anyhow. I just want one of them sammiches that Anna bought all up."

Morgan turned and looked at Anna. She'd just fed the last few pieces to the girls, and by the looks of them, to their face, hair, and dresses too. Morgan could not believe how much he loved these kids. He looked back at Junior and told him that they were all gone.

"That just ain't right, you know. I fucking wanted—" Morgan punched him in the face. Not hard, just enough to knock him back on his ass. "What the hell was that for, you fucking turd?"

"Turd? Well, it was for cursing around my children. I don't condone that." Junior looked confused again. "I don't allow people to curse around them. That's what condone means."

"I knows that." Sure he did. And he was a scholar of the highest degree too. "You could 'a just said, 'don't be cussing around my kids.' There weren't no reason for you to be hitting me like that."

"But my way was so much more fun." Morgan put out his hand and laughed when Junior flinched from it. "I was offering you my hand to help you up."

"I think I'll just be staying here while we finish this up. You gots yourself some cash on you? I was thinking that you could spot me some until I can get the money that Dad stashed away for me." Morgan told him no. "It's not like it's gonna hurt you none. I just have to be able to get me a meal or two and be sleeping in a real bed for a while. Just help me out. You should anyway. I could be helpful to you."

"How do you figure that?" Junior told him of his plan. "I see. You want me to support you in a lifestyle that you wish while you hunt down the money that your father and your brothers stole from a bank with your help, and you'll give me half of it. How is that going to set with the rest of your family?"

"You'll have to deal with them, I'm a' guessing. Besides, I'm thinking that after today, they'll both not be getting out anytime soon. Not to mention, they ain't nearly as smart as I am." Morgan rolled his eyes. "You don't believe that I'm smart? I am. I'm the only ones of us that finished up middle school."

"Well, then, I guess you are pretty smart, aren't you?" Morgan decided to find out what he could. "How the hell did you get out of prison? Did you have to pay someone to get your ass out when you were no way near your time to be released?"

"Nah, I got no money. But what I do gots is smarts." Morgan asked him what he'd done again. "So I fixed it so that my roomie was nearly dead. He was getting on my last nerve anyhow. So I strangled him enough so that he'd have to go to the infirmary. After he gets himself there and keels over, I real casual like just slip in the bed that he was dead in and tossed his body in the pressure thing. It smashed his body up like he was nothing more than a coconut, I tell you. They think I'm dead now, so I just go out with the rest of the bodies. 'Course, I had to lay real still, and when they dumped me in the back with the rest of the real dead ones, I didn't make no noises when they roughed me up a bit."

"How did they account for you not being in your bed?" Junior told him it didn't matter none to him on account 'a him being free. "I see. So you escaped prison because you murdered a man by crushing his body in a compactor."

"Yeah, that's the name of that thing. You sure know a lot of words. I bet you never have a lick of trouble with cross ways puzzles or nothing, do you?" Morgan said that he was a college professor. "Oh yeah? Well, I guess it takes all kinds. So, we gots a deal?"

"No, we *gots* nothing. First of all, you're a criminal. Secondly, and I guess this shouldn't surprise me, you escaped from prison and you have no idea where the money is. Am I right so far?" Junior said that he had himself a clue where it might be. "Then why aren't you going to get it?"

"It's a fair piece away from here." Morgan wondered if he were to take the man to the money, would that give the police enough to take him back to prison. But he wasn't sure who on the force had been in on Junior getting out, and Morgan wondered if they'd call about him escaping. But he was becoming a nuisance, and he wanted the fucker in prison now. "You take me out there and I'll divide it up right then and there. You can even do some recounting if you've a mind to."

He asked for time to think about it. When he was told that he could, Morgan went to sit down with his family. Anna was stressed, but when he winked at her, she smiled. It was tight, sure, but he'd take whatever she was willing to give him.

Are you all right? She nodded, then shook her head. Junior left them, laughing when he went on his way. When he was out of ear shot, Morgan spoke to Anna again. "I have an idea how we can get him back in prison. I know that you were made aware that we wanted him there without chance of parole. I think I might have it. I hope so anyway."

"I just don't understand why he wasn't arrested when he killed that woman." He told her that the cameras were not for public use, and it would get Rogen in trouble. "I know, she told me that too. But even standing up to him is getting harder and harder. I'm terrified for our kids."

"He knows where the cash is." Anna asked what cash. "The money from the bank robbery. They could never prove that the four of them were in on it, so they only got life. They'd been smart enough—probably took all four of them— to cut off the cameras. As it is, they could all get out with good behavior. Or worse yet, like Junior did. He even told me how he did that."

"What does he want in return? I'm sure that he has some grand plan that is going to make you both rich." Morgan smiled at her as he ate his ice cream. "You're going to do whatever he wants? That's not like you."

"It's not. But if it will get him off the streets, then I'm for anything it takes to get him out of your life." She smiled at him. "Yes, you get it now, don't you? We're going to take him down."

Chapter 7

Thatcher didn't much care for Rogen and Anna being in on this one. There was too much at stake. While Rogen wouldn't be there in actuality, she was still going to be commanding a bunch of people that might get Anna hurt. But since no one had asked him, he was being wise and not saying a word. While the ladies were making plans for their part in the capture and arrest of Noah Junior, he and his brothers were working on the set up with the funeral home that had released not just Junior, but it looked like forty other inmates.

"You're drifting again." Thatcher told Beckett he was sorry. "This is going to be epic; don't you think? I mean, we're finding out so much about this funeral home that I'm surprised no one has ever looked into it before. Might make a good story."

"Only you would think that. And we're not calling the newspaper at all. First of all, we can't have Rogen's location out there. Not to mention, we don't want anyone getting any ideas on how to make this work for them and other funeral homes." Beckett told him that he was aware of it. "I'm sorry. I'm just stressed a little. To think that this place has been in business since our dad was just a kid. Do we know yet how long they've been doing this?"

"Only since the son took over from his father about ten years ago." He asked Jonas if they were sure it was just the son. "I am. About ten years before Mr. Williams died, he took out a loan on the place. Then about six months after his death, Parker Williams, his only son, pays off both mortgages, as well as has the place renovated. I was happy to help him out with that for the bank, but now I'm wondering how he was able to gather up the money. I thought it was insurance, but that doesn't work out either. Who is paying him? Or a better question would be, how is he being paid? There is no influx of cash that I can find when I go over his books. Something isn't right here."

"Okay, so we know that the funeral home is in on this scam, or whatever we're calling it. The list of things that we don't know about this thing is much longer than what we do know." Thatcher agreed with Houston when the rest of them did. "So we do this one step at a time. First of all, we know that someone on the inside is guilty as fuck too, simply because of the extra body that goes out when they're collected. What I don't understand is, why are they holding the dead until they get a bunch of them? For that matter, how are they holding them?"

"I found that." He looked at Beckett. "You're not going to like this any better than knowing that they do it. The only freezer they have is the one that they store the food in. And with that knowledge, I can about tell you when a body is going out. They cut back on the amount of meat and frozen things to make room for the bodies. When there is a large order for groceries placed, you know that they're going to get rid of their storage of the dead."

"That is the most disgusting thing that I've ever heard of." Beckett said that there was more. "Do I want to know?"

"More than likely not. But it looks to me like some of these bodies that actually die for whatever reason might not be shipped out ever. In the last sixteen months, several men have come up missing, but were reported found after the state went in and did a surprise inspection of the place. What do you suppose they're doing with the bodies?" Thatcher got it first, and he said there was no way in hell that was legal. "Of course it's not. But feeding the inmates the dead is a perfect way to rid themselves of the extra...meat, I guess you could call it."

"Christ, this is much worse than we ever thought." Jonas said that would also cut the cost of having to feed them very much. Thatcher was a surgeon, but this sort of thing was making even him ill. "So how far up the ladder does this shit go? I mean, to the top, you figure?"

"I think so. At least the person who is doing the ordering would think that something is off. Then there are the people that would have to make sure that death certificates are filed on the living that leave. This thing is so complicated that it's small wonder no one has figured it out." Jonas had another point. "Are some of the inmates in on this, you think?"

Thatcher asked what happened to the list of people working there. When he was handed it, he looked it over. He started putting numbers next to the people that worked in the kitchen, the infirmary, as well as the head of the prison.

"We need the bank records of all these men. Also, try and

find out where the money might be going if it's not in the local bank." He divided up the list. "I'll work on the list for the kitchen with Jonas. You four divide the list in two again and work on that. Banking first, or at least an influx of money at any time of the month."

While they were starting on their list, he called for Rogen. She came into the room where they were working and showed them the password to get into the national banking system. After that, it was easy to go down the list and not only figure out who was in on this, but also the people that were shipping money to another country. Two hours after starting, they were all finished with their lists.

"All of them. Every person that works there has a part in this scam. I suppose they'd have to be. I mean, how would any one person or group of people be able to keep something like this on the quiet side?" Thatcher looked at this list again. "But who is—?"

"I got it." They all turned to Dawson when he started to whoop it up. "I not only know who is paying them off, but how. Christ, this was just as simple as the last diagnosis I had when Mrs. Emery brought her daughter in. It's not the family, like I first thought, but the groups that they worked for. Mobsters, as well as gangs that employed these men. Look at what I found on this check here. It's from one of the biggest mobsters in our state. There are checks like this from all over the place, from different groups that need their hitmen back. Even checks from gangs that I've never heard of before."

It was a certified check made out to one of the prison guards. After they knew how to look for that, they each looked over the accounts on their list and found the same sorts of checks. On each one of the checks, in the corner of it where *memo* was printed, it said "refund from a credit card." There were at least ten of those on each and every account.

"The bank didn't notice because it looks like they cashed them in different places around the state. You can see how they were cashed on the back. Since it's a certified check, they're pretty much guaranteed their money back." Thatcher was proud of himself for figuring that out. "If you look, I'm betting that they have a list of places that they'd cashed these checks so as not to go back there a second time. This is, I have to admit, brilliant on someone's part."

The next checks they investigated were those of the funeral home. The only one being paid there was Parker, and he was making a killing off this. All he had to do was bring all the bodies in and let them go. He had no overhead at all, and was making about twenty grand on each person that was brought to his establishment.

"So, how do we prove this?" Dad had a good question. Thatcher didn't know the answer, but he was sure that he could get some help from someone. Asking Rogen if she could join them, he could see that she did not look happy about being interrupted.

"I have shit I'm doing. Why do you all look like you've had a nice tasty meal? What did you do?" Thatcher showed her what they'd figured out between them, then told her what they needed. "We can't prove anything for the moment. Since Junior was released this way, someone will figure out that their scam has been found out. They might not stop fucking around with the dead right away, but it will put them on alert, and that will fuck up your catch. As large as yours will be, it would be a shame not to get the cocksucker in prison right along with the inmates that they'd been feeding ground Joey

99

to, or whoever they ground up to give them in the way of hamburger. Christ, that is really going to have a lot of people puking in their oats, don't you think?"

The two arrests groups—or really three, Rogen told him—would have to be arrested at the same time or they'd lose out on some of them. The prison and the funeral home would have to be done first. If not, then they'd miss catching one. Then they could arrest Junior for his part in a great many things.

Rogen told them all she thought they'd done a fantastic job other than annoying the fuck out of her. When she walked away, Thatcher saw each of his brothers high five the other. Their first undercover job search, and they'd found shit out that he never, not in a million plus years, would have guessed. Rogen made about a dozen phone calls before she was ready to make the move on the two places. There were other elements involved in this capture and arrest, things that he wouldn't be a part of, but he so did love watching her work. She was professional, loud, and cursed like someone who might have written the books on it. But Thatcher loved her with all his body and soul.

The FBI would need to be involved, as well as a lot of other agencies, she told him, simply because they were all going to want a piece of what was going on. Rogen also told him that no one could know that they'd been a part of it.

"They'll believe that you guys might have known all along. Not so much about the people getting out, but the fact that they were using humans as their supper. Cannibalism is going to have a great many people protesting things that have nothing to do with what you unearthed." He asked her what. "For instance, there will be a lot of prisoners that demand to be released because of this. As much as I hate to admit it, there might be a few that get out. Then there is the backlash about the funerals that were legitimate. Like my father's, for instance. Did they really do what they were supposed to? Shit like that."

"It might even tarnish the name of Parker Williams's father." Rogen nodded. "There is nothing we can do to keep that from happening, is there?"

"I can do a little on the side, but people will do what they do best. Take a story and make it all about them and how something hurt them. I would expect to see a lot of lawsuits about all of this. Not just the funeral home, but also the prison. Then there are the people that were eaten. We might not ever be able to figure that out." He asked her if she thought no one would want to do this. "Oh, they'll do this all right. It's exposure. Another thing people like to see is when someone is handed their ass. A lot of people will be too. Not just the men you found, but I'm betting that there will be a lot more named in all this. It's going to open and close a great many cases."

"Christ, I never thought of that. Wives and children of these men involved; they're going to be blamed for being in on it as well." Rogen said that they more than likely knew something was going on, just not the details. "Right. I wouldn't want to know either. A lot of shit is going to hit the fan, isn't it?"

"Yes, but don't ever think this was a bad thing, Thatcher. You and your family did a great job of not only keeping people from continuing to be released without reason, but you've also found the money and where it was going, and you know to the dollar how much was paid out by each person that wanted them released. That, to me, is the best. A lot of heads are going to be chopped off with this one." He nodded, but could only think how this was going to affect a lot of innocents. "This is why I don't like names when I'm to take out a target. It's much easier to just simply think of them as scum or trash. I sleep better at nights."

By midnight, his house was full of men and women with letters on their jackets or vests. They were being brought with logos on their vans or cars as painters, gardeners, as well as caterers. Rogen said that they'd need to have a large outdoor picnic for the town later that would make the people being here now more plausible. So no one in town would ever think why they were going to such extremes for no reason.

Thatcher told his mom what he needed her to do for him. She, of course, thought it was a splendid idea. Not the arrests, but that she could plan a party big enough to treat the town, and on the government's dime. The rest, he was glad to know, she wanted nothing to do with.

Wondering what she'd want to serve as meat, he decided that for a little while, he was going to eat only greens — salads and such. Thatcher wasn't sure that his belly could take much meat at the moment. All of this was just too fresh to him.

~*~

Morgan had to admit that he was nervous about his part in all this. He might not have agreed at all except for the people that were going to be at the cemetery where the money was hidden. Being able to communicate with Rogen and Thatcher about where he was taking Moron, his new name for Junior, made it so much easier for them to get there before he pulled in. He did think it was horrible that they'd actually used their own mother's gravesite for a place to hide the money. Moron was singing to the radio when Morgan reached over and turned it off.

"Hey, I was listening at that." Morgan, with his car bugged all over with camera and microphones, had to remind himself not to talk loudly. "What's up your ass anyway? Didn't I tell you that you could count out your share before we even leave there?"

"Yes, you did. Several times. I have a question for you. But don't strain your head in trying to figure out a lie. I'll know. I can smell it when you do." He could, but with Moron, he couldn't get past the smell of his unwashed body. "You never said to me how much my cut was going to be."

That was something that Rogen and crew wanted to know before he and Moron got there. It would narrow down for them all which bank robbery Moron was talking about. So far as he knew there was only one. But they had four unsolved bank robberies, and they wanted to know which one to pin on them.

"Millions." Morgan didn't even glance at him. "Whenever we'd get us a good haul, like a bank or some fucking shit, we'd take it to the cemetery when we didn't get caught and hide it right there where Momma was buried. After a while, Daddy decided that if we left it there until things cooled off, then they'd not be able to pin them on us."

"What happened that it's still there? Nothing came up for you?" Moron said that was exactly the issuance, like that even made sense. Then he told him. "So, you never really got to spend much of it because you were never allowed to go and pick up the cash on your own. One of you were always in prison for something else."

"Yeah, that's it. If we was caught there by the others then

they'd be allowed to murder us off. We made us a package, you see. We sticked our self to it to no matter how much we wanted to just take a little biddy bit of it." Morgan asked if they trusted each other. "I didn't trust any of them but Daddy. And I knew that he'd bring down a world of hurts on me that I might wish to die from."

Morgan knew that everyone was listening in on this, and right now were more than likely setting up to take the man in. This was the first step to take down a bunch of thieves, as well as murderers. After this, he'd be out of the circle of things that were going to happen later today.

It was decided that Moron would have to be taken in first. Then later, before anyone got wind of what was going on, they'd hit both the prison and Parker Williams's home and place of business at the same time. Neither place was close to each other. The prison was upstate, and the funeral home was about fifty miles from where they all lived. Morgan knew that Anna was sitting at home with his mom, and that she was scared that he was going to get hurt in some way. He was too, but he'd put on a brave face for her before leaving the house. Anna hadn't believed it for a minute.

"You be careful, or so help me, Morgan, I will hunt you down and rip you a new ass. I kid you not on this." He kissed her on the nose. "You're not going to get away with that either. I want you to promise me that you're not going to be hurt. I can't stand the thought of you out there with that idiot."

"I love you to pieces, Anna, but I can't promise you that. What if I get knocked down when they arrest him? I fall on a piece of sharp—I don't know, grass or something, and cut myself. You'll hurt me if I make a promise and then break it." She said she was going to hit him. "That reminds me of a question that I had for you. Do you have any idea why Rogen hits people when she's talking to them?"

"They're morons?" He said that he didn't think his dad was. "It's to get his attention away from whatever he was thinking about at the time. Mostly she does it because she can, I think. But really, it's to draw a person's attention to her and not whatever shitty thoughts they're having. It's violent, yes it is, but it also works. Don't change the subject. You know how nervous I am about this."

"I do. I promise you that I do." He held her to him and felt from her all the love that a man could ever want. "I can promise you that I won't die out there. Not unless I really do fall and hit my head on the headstone. I have enough hardware on my person that I think I weigh at least forty more pounds than I did this morning. I love you, Anna, and I will try my very best not to get harmed while I'm working with these men."

She told him that was the best she could hope for, then kissed him again. Now here he was, in the car with one of the biggest idiots that he'd ever had to be around. He knew that Moron had a gun, something that he hadn't told Anna on purpose. However, it wasn't loaded. Not to mention, Moron also didn't know that you needed silver to kill a shifter. Morgan tried very hard not to think of him shooting him in the head.

When they pulled into the cemetery, the little mic in his ear spoke to him. Nearly screaming at Rogen to not do that again, he listened while she told him what was going on around him.

"There are two funerals going on around you. One about half a football field away to your right. The other one is just

105

about four headstones away from you. Both are fake, and are there to keep your ass from getting hurt." He thanked her. "I have to tell you, your fucking wife came in here and threatened me about ten minutes ago. Morgan, I'm going to convince her to work with me if it's the last thing I do. Damn, but she's ballsy. I like her more than you, and I like you a great deal. All right, listen up. Just walk to the grave as if you know what the fuck you're doing."

I haven't any idea what the fuck I'm doing. Or how the hell you talked me into this. She said that she'd not had to. *No, you sent my brother after me. That is playing unfairly.*

"A girl's gotta do what a girl's gotta do. Can you see the headstone yet?" He said he was near it. "Don't dig the grave if you can help it. Tell dumbass that you drove or some shit like that."

That was just what he told Moron when he insisted that he dig up the money. "I've been carting your ass around since I picked you up this morning. Taking you all over town to get supplies. I would have thought you'd have everything you needed before I got you." Moron grumbled about how he was older than him. "I don't give two shits if you're geriatric. I'm not digging that up."

"What the hell does that mean?" Counting to ten first, Morgan told him that it was someone over eighty. "Why the hell don't you just say that instead of using big fancy words all the time? Your momma must be pissed off at you all the time for making her feel stupid. Are you showing off to me? You don't gotta. I'm not impressed by you anymore than you are me. I'll dig it, but I'm charging you for this. It comes out of your part."

Not even bothering to answer him, Morgan sat down on

the grass to wait. Moron had to pull the money out of the grave or it was all for naught. As he waited, he looked around, wondering if there were any spaces left in this cemetery.

It had been around longer than he had been. His great grandmother was around here somewhere, he thought. He'd have to look it up. Morgan decided that he was going to ask Anna if she would help him pick out a place for them so that someday he'd not have to leave this burden to his children.

The responsibility had gone to his parents when Mom's parents had passed away. They'd had no money back then, only an idea of how much it would cost. No one expected it to be as expensive as it was. At least that was what he'd overheard his parents telling Mom's brother, Jake, when he'd asked her how come she'd not gone all out for the funeral.

"Because we're going to have to make payments for as long as we live as it is now. Where is your part in all this?" Jake had asked Mom what she meant by that. "She was your mother too, the last time that I looked. How much are you going to pay me a month to have made all these arrangements for this?"

"You made the arrangements without asking me. You pay for it. What I asked you, and don't think that I didn't notice that you didn't answer, was how come you only got a single day of showing and then burial. Why cheap out on Mom?" She told him that she couldn't afford it. "Whatever. Do you know when they're going to read the will? I'd like to get my share of the money and get out of town. If she left us both the house, you can buy me out. I don't want anything to do with anything that isn't hard cold cash."

Mom was pissed off at him for the rest of the day. How the hell was she supposed to buy him out of anything? As it turned out, not only did Mom get everything in the will, but the house as well. Which, sadly, they had to sell in order to pay off the funeral, as making another monthly payment wouldn't have been very easy for them at the time. There was a letter with the will for Uncle Jake that Mom was to hand to him if he stirred up any trouble.

Uncle Jake sued Mom a few days after the will was read. As his name was not mentioned in the will, he'd not been notified when it had been read. At the courthouse, Mom had handed the letter to her attorney, who in turn made copies for everyone involved. Jake had been so angry that his own mother had kept an accounting of all the things that he'd stolen off her, as well as all the money that he'd borrowed and never repaid, that he had yet to come around again. Good riddance to him.

"Woo hoo, here it is." Morgan was dragged from his memories when Moron spoke. "Just where it's supposed to be, right here on top of Mom's grave. Dad said it was the perfect place to keep it on account 'a she couldn't spend it. And she would have too."

The money was in bank bags, four of them, with the names of the banks that were robbed blazed right across the front of them. Just as Moron was pulling out his gun, to no doubt kill his partner, the agencies that were there to arrest him jumped in and saved him from having to explain to Anna how he'd gotten shot.

"There will be a gag put on him, and he'll be kept in an undisclosed location. That way, no one will hear about it until we're ready for them to." Donaldson, Rogen's direct report, shook Morgan's hand. "You did well, Morgan. Your family should be very proud of you. Rogen said that this was all your idea too. Thank you for that. A lot of insurance companies will be settled up now that we've been able to catch the Hayes men. This will have repercussions on the rest of them in the prison system too."

"I'm just glad that I was able to help you all." Donaldson thanked him again.

As he was making his way to the car, he watched Moron being read his rights and then cuffed. He was screaming the entire time that he'd been bear trapped. Whatever the hell that meant.

Chapter 8

Meggie rocked Renee until she was asleep. The little girl had bumped her head when trying her best to climb up the coffee table. While she'd been comforting her little granddaughter, Thatch had been talking about how they had to child proof the house. Meggie agreed with him—there was a lot of things out that a little child could get harmed on. Especially the coffee table.

"I never did like that thing anyway." She said that it had come with the end tables, and they both had liked them. "Yeah, I do like them for a cup of tea or something, but that table, it's been bumped one too many times now. I say we either pad it with something or get another one. Whatcha think, honey?"

"I'm thinking that we could use a whole new set of living room things. I only just realized that this couch set is about twenty years old. And I don't need to remind you that it has one of those nasty springs in the middle seat." Thatch remembered by rubbing his bottom. "What if you got on our computer and found us some nicer things, Thatch? I just love the set that Morgan has in his home now. It's so plush that when you sit in it, it's difficult to stay awake."

Thatch was firing up their computer then. Even it was old enough that it wouldn't even update anymore. She'd have to have one of the boys work on getting them one of those as well. Laying little Renee on the floor with her sister to nap, she checked on Eddie and went to the computer with Thatch. She fell in love with the very first thing he pulled up.

"We'd have to go and check it out, you know." She nodded, but still liked it. "For all we know, it could be as hard as my head, and about as useless too."

Meggie smacked him on the shoulder. "You know you're useful to me, you old poop. I love it when Rogen calls you that for some reason. It suits you." Thatch admitted that he liked it as well, but not to tell Rogen that. "Oh no, I won't. She is such a hoot, don't you think?"

"I do. Anna is too, I'm thinking. I heard Rogen telling Thatcher the other day that she thought that Anna could whoop her butt if it came to it. Something about street smarts or something. You think she's right? Not that I want them to tussle over anything—they scare me a bit." Meggie told him that they both scared her a little. "But they love us, so I'm thinking that we don't have much to worry about with them."

"We should make a day of going shopping, Thatch. Just you and me, running around town, and then having us a nice supper there while we're at it." He said that he loved that idea. "Then tomorrow, let's do it. This thing with that young hooligan will be finished, and we're going to be safe from him coming here. There is that thing with the other places, but we're not involved in that, are we?"

"Just Rogen on that. She sure is happy that Anna was helping her with this stuff. Said it might have taken her a day or two longer to figure it out, but she'd have gotten there." They were both laughing when the phone rang. "I'll be getting it. Why, if it's one of them robot calls I'm not going to be too happy with them."

She could have corrected him, but she didn't get the chance. Whoever it was or whatever they had to tell him, Meggie could tell that he was upset about it. When he held out the phone for her to take, she shook her head.

"You have to take it, Meggie love. He's a wanting to talk to you." She said no. "Please, darling. I'll be right here with you. I promise you. Come on now. It's your brother Jake."

That was all it took for her to be all fired up. Taking the phone from her husband, she put it to her ear. She could hear people in the background talking about money and fines. Whatever Jake had gotten himself into, she was having no part of it. He'd not hurt her like that again. When she said hello she could hear the relief in Jakes voice.

"Oh, Meggie. I'm so glad that I caught you at home. I need for you to sell whatever you have and come bring me some cash. Don't fuck around on me with this — just do what I tell you. It's a lot of money, so you'll have to maybe sell off your house or something to gather it up. I'll meet you at the plane with the cash" She asked him what was going on. "I got myself in over my head. Just like Mom used to tell you about me. She usually bailed me out, but now that she's gone and you got all her shit, then you can do it for me. I'll need you to hurry, however. Don't lollygag around on this. I need about a hundred thousand to get me in the black again, then more for a bit of walking around cash. A man like me cannot be without funds. So you remember that when you start bitching about how you can't get it for me."

"Why don't you get a job, Jake? I keep my nose clean, unlike you. I work my but off all the time." Jake said that he was clean right now. "Right now? You make it sound like you weren't this morning."

"Don't be preaching to me, Meggie. We both know that you fucked me up by telling Mom that she needed to keep better records of shit that she lent me. And that shouldn't have been part of the things that she didn't leave me either. That was my inheritance. Nothing to do with me not paying her back." Meggie told him that he'd never paid her back. "So? It's not like she wasn't good for it. And besides, the house is sold now, so I can't even say that they can use that to get me out of this mess. I blame you for this too. You should have shared with me no matter what her will said."

Meggie thought about what he was saying to her and why she was letting him. Then she thought of her daughters in law and how they would have handled this. Nodding her head, she came to a decision that she knew was a step in the right direction in dealing with her brother. Cut him off and out of her life once and for all.

"I tell you what, Jake. I'll come to where you are and work on what you're telling me." She thought that was vague enough that he'd think that she was helping him out. "It will take me a couple of days to make the arrangements."

"No, that won't work. You have to get your ass in gear now, Meggie. No stalling on this. Now that you've seen the way things should have been all along, you'll need to bring me half of everything that you got from the will, including any profit you got when you sold Mom's house. In cash. No checks. I don't trust you enough to not put a stop on the check. Cash, all of it."

"Yes, half of everything that I ended up with as an inheritance. I can do that." She started calculating in her head, and realized this was going to be better than she thought it would be. "I'll even bring out the paperwork on what things cost, all right? That way you will know that I didn't cheat you, as you said that I did."

"I have to say, Meggie, it certainly took you long enough to get your head out of your ass. Christ, it's been too long in coming. I should charge you for that too, but I'll be generous to you this one time. You should also remember that I'm older than you, and that I should be able to get a part of what you got. I might just have to hit you up for that later." She didn't say anything, but let him ramble on. "All right. Today or else. I swear, Meggie, I'm not going to put up with your fucking bullshit anymore."

"Oh, you won't have to." She smiled and looked at Thatch as she hung up on Jake while he was still talking. "I need to make arrangements to go to Jake. I'm going to end this once and for all. I was thinking that I'd just take Rogen and Anna with me, but I think we should make this a trip for us all. What do you think?"

"Do you know where he is?" The phone rang in that moment, and she knew that it was going to be her brother. Thatch was laughing as she answered.

"You're still the biggest dumbass that ever lived, Meggie. Get a pen and paper. Or a crayon—I guess you have those brats still around." She told him she was ready and wrote down the address that he gave her. "Don't forget it. I don't want to have to listen to you whine about shit either. Cash,

Meggie. Don't make me have to take you to task for this. You know that I can and will hurt you."

"So you think. Goodbye, Jake." She hung up the phone and went to find her mate. Did Jake actually think that the boys had never grown up? It would be just like him to think that if he didn't have anything to do with it, the world did not go on.

Reaching out to her family, she asked if they'd accompany her on a trip. Everyone was willing to go — most of them had dealt with Jake for her before. Well, today she was going to stand up on her own two feet, and make sure that the fucking bastard got what was coming to him.

For the last several years, since he'd learned that he was getting nothing from their mom's estate, he'd been hounding her about money. She never gave in to him, knowing, she supposed, that it would never end if she did. He'd drain her and her family dry if she gave him one nickel.

Going through her files, she was glad now that she'd kept all the paperwork together on the selling of the estate. Bills that the money was used for, and how much she and the family had had to pay out of pocket for what the sale of the house didn't cover. She would never have thought in a million years that a funeral could cost so much.

The house had sold for a good bit of money, but Mom had taken a loan against the house in order to put in a new furnace, as well as a new roof. It had made proceeds from the sale of the house more, but she'd had to pay that loan off before she was able to get the money from the sale. That had barely covered the funeral. There was just enough, with them adding in a bit of their own, to get a nice marker for Mom and Dad. Something that they'd never been able to afford before.

She laughed when she figured out how much money she'd had to pay to cover all the expenses of the funeral. Even as cheaply as they'd gone, they'd had to come up with about four hundred dollars more to cover it all. In her estimations, Jake owed her about two hundred dollars. That would be what he would have gotten as half the money — him owing her.

She was startled to see Rogen in the living room with Thatch when she entered. She'd been there, it looked like, since she'd gotten off the phone with Jake. Rogen asked her to have a seat. Smiling, she sat down.

"I heard about your brother a few weeks ago. I wanted to tell you about him before you went out there." Meggie asked if it was bad. "Yes."

"Oh. I knew that he wasn't a nice person. He wasn't as a child. As he got older, he seemed to think that the world revolved around him and his demands. What has he gotten into?"

"*If* you go out there — and I don't believe that you should — he will drag you into what he has going on." Meggie wouldn't go if this woman thought that she shouldn't. "I'll go. I think you should let the professionals handle this."

"Is it that bad?" Rogen only nodded. "Are you not telling me because you don't think that I can handle it, or because you simply don't want me to know?"

"He's part of a racketeering outfit that is trafficking young women, as young as ten, around the world. The reason he wants you to come out there today is because he is going to sell you off, then use that money to invest in another load of girls that he's kidnapped." Meggie didn't even ask her if she was sure. She'd learned that if Rogen told you something, it was as sure as it could be. "Will you let me handle this?"

"Yes. But, if you don't mind, I'd like to be there after he's arrested. I'm assuming that you'll do that rather than kill him off." Rogen said that she wasn't sure what would have to happen to him if he didn't come in willingly. "He won't. All right. I'll stay here and play with my grandbabies. You let me know only if he's dead or alive, and I'll decide what to do then."

"I love you, Meggie. I want you to know that."

The hug was just what she needed to break the dam of tears. As she sobbed about how mean he'd been to her as a child, Rogen held her. It was the most comforting thing that she'd had in a long while.

~*~

Jake couldn't believe that he and his sister were from the same gene pool. She was about as stupid as stupid could be. Smiling, he wondered how much he'd get for her, and would bet that she'd let herself go. But so long as she was worth the one hundred thousand that he needed, he didn't care what she looked like.

The schedule that she'd given him for the arrival of the plane was right on time. As he waited for her to come up the long carpeted area from the disembarking zone, Jake thought about her as a child. She'd forever been under his feet and in his business. He thought that was why he hated her so much. Meggie told on him every time he had a little fun.

As people started moving off the plane, he watched the two young women as they walked toward him like they owned the place. There were a couple of men with them, big men that he recognized right away were tigers. There wasn't any possible way that either of these women was his sister.

She'd never looked that good on her best days.

"Mr. Jake Simons?" He nodded, and one of them smiled at him. "We're here in place of Meggie Robinson. She just couldn't make it."

Christ, he thought, he was going to make a killing off two women. They were stunners, and the fact that both of them were cats would only make men want them all the more. As he looked them up and down, he felt rather than saw the two men with them move around him. When Jake reached out to touch one of the women's cheeks, he cried out in pain when he was suddenly in a neck hold.

"I might have not mentioned that you're not to touch us, but this was so much more fun for me." She nodded behind him, and he found himself free, but still on the nasty carpet of the airport. "I'm Rogen Robinson. This is my sister-in-law Anna. You might remember your nephews, Morgan and Thatcher. Thatcher is my mate and husband. Morgan is the same to Anna."

"There isn't any way that you're related to me." She said she felt the same way about him. There was something there, something he couldn't quite put his finger on, but he let it go for now. "She was coming here to bring me cash. Do you have it? I hope to Christ so. I don't have time for this bullshit."

"Cash? No, I'm afraid not. What she said she'd bring you is an accounting of the money. Half of everything that she ended up with as an inheritance, I believe is what she told you." Again, something wasn't right, but he wanted this done now so he could get to the auction house sooner rather than later. It mattered little to him how much the inheritance was now. He had this bitch to sell, and he was going to be on easy street for some time now. "I've made arrangements for us to

119

get together in a meeting room here. That way things can be settled and I can go back home on the next flight."

Like hell she was. The men could—he had no use for them. Jake wasn't even afraid of them trying to hurt him. He was their flesh and blood, and there were rules about that. Smiling now that things were going to go his way for a change, he followed them to the room that had a reserved sign on it. Pulling that off as she entered, he was nearly giddy as he sat down in one of the chairs.

"Now. Here we go. This is the cost of the funeral, as well as the head stone—" He cut her off, telling her that he wasn't paying anything on that half assed funeral. "Shut the fuck up, and don't interrupt me again or you will face the consequences. As I was saying, here is the cost of the funeral, headstone, as well as the cost of the gravesite opening and closing. As well as the flowers and the cost of the services. Half assed or not, nothing is cheap in any of this."

"Are you finished now? I can speak?" Rogen nodded, and he wanted to slap the shit out of her. But damaging either one of them now would show up when he put her before the people he'd had lined up for his sister. "I'm not paying anything on that funeral. She was to bring me cash for what she made from the sale of the house, and half of everything else that she got and I didn't."

"That's what we're here for. You still owe her two hundred bucks. Like you didn't trust her, she doesn't trust you either, so we'll take that in—"

"Listen, bitch, you will get this straight, or I'm going to kick the shit—"

Again he was in a head lock, but it wasn't the men that were holding him, but Anna, the other woman. Christ, she was so tiny that he'd never dream that she could hold him, much less hold him this tightly. Struggling only made her tighten her grip about his neck. Jake was beginning to see stars when he was finally freed.

Thatcher and Morgan hadn't moved. In fact, it looked to him like they were bored out of their minds. He laughed when he pointed to them. They both looked up when he said their names.

"You're so fucking lazy that you'd allow your wives to try and hurt me? What sort of pussies did my sister raise? I swear to Christ, I'm going to take her on when I finally get to see her again." Anna said that he wasn't. Jake looked at her. "I'm not what?"

"Going to see her again. Not as long as I live you won't. I wanted to kill you as soon as we stepped off the plane, but I was told that I had to behave. This is me behaving and not killing your fucking ass right now." Jake glanced at the men when Anna jerked his head around to face her. "When I'm speaking, you will look at me, dumbass. Now, fork over your part of the money or I'm going to take it from you. Cash or ass, I don't care, but I'm going to take something back to Meggie."

This wasn't going at all like he wanted it to, and that too he was going to blame on his sister. Meggie had been a pain in his ass since the day she'd been born. He was going to get back at her if it was the last thing he did.

Just as he was opening his mouth to demand to talk to his sister, several armed men came into the room. Military. It was the first thing that popped into his head, and it stayed there when they drew their weapons and put them at their sides. They made no bones about the fact that they were there for him, and he felt his balls curl up around his neck, so much so that he had to clear his throat twice before he was able to speak. But Rogen beat him to it.

"The auction house that you were planning to attend is, even as we speak, being raided. All the bidders there are being arrested, and even the ones that you have in your computer are being picked up at their homes or places of business. You made it very easy for me to figure out who else would be in on your plans." He asked her what she was talking about. "The auction house where you would auction off the children and young women that you kidnapped all over the United States. You can imagine how their families are feeling about you right now. And the men that you brought into the place. Everyone is celebrating."

"I have no idea what you're taking about." Thatcher got up and handed him a tablet looking thing. Right there on the screen was exactly what Rogen had told him. The place was overrun with not just police, but every agency that he'd been trying to avoid since he'd left home. "I don't know why you'd think that I'd have anything to do with something as barbaric as this."

Thatcher took the pad back and fiddled with it for a moment. When he took it back from him, the sound was on and he could see his procurement boss talking. He was not only spilling the beans about what went on at the place, but that he himself, Jake Simons, was completely in charge of the entire operation.

"I don't know that man either. I'm guessing this is a scheme of my sister's to get out of paying me what she owes me. Well, you can tell her for me that I'm not going to put up with this anymore. I'm going to take this to a higher court." Rogen and Anna laughed. "What the fuck do you find so funny?"

"We were able to follow the money to your offshore accounts. It was another thing that I must thank you for—leaving all your notes and passwords right there beside your computer was brilliant. Well, not on your part, but it was very helpful to me." Jake asked Anna what she'd been doing in his home. "Looking for shit that would take you down. It was easy, as I said, because you left all the information right there for us to find. Thanks."

"That money is mine for my retirement years. You can't touch that." Anna told him that she'd not only touched it, but she'd taken all of it. "You fucking cunt. I'm going to kill you."

He moved, but the men in the room did too. Just as he was reaching for Anna's throat, he stopped. The guns, all of them, were pointed right at his head. The little red lights coming from them looked like he was a pincushion that was letting out enough light to power a town.

"This is going to be what happens to you. And if you interrupt me, I'm going to stand up and leave here with my family, and you'll be left to these men to do whatever they would like." Rogen leaned in and whispered to him, and he flinched. "Anna is still going home with something of yours. What will it be? You must decide now, because I have a feeling that you're not going to last long after today."

"Don't kill me. Please, I beg of you. I'll do whatever it is you want. Anything within reason, I mean. I do have to live after this." Anna laughed and told him that everything was going to be provided for him if he were to tell the truth. "I will. I promise you I will. I want my money back too."

He had to give her a list of names of his investors. Jake didn't have a problem with that. He knew if they were in the same seat as he was right now they'd turn him over without any problems. Pulling out his phone, he gave her not only their names, but phone numbers as well. It was the least he could do since he was going to be taken care of and get his money all back.

There were other questions too. About how long had he been doing this? What was his profit margin? Things like that. Then Anna asked him what his plans had been for his sister. So far, he'd told them nothing but the truth. Jake didn't have any trouble continuing on that roll since he knew that he was going to get Meggie sooner or later. Once he set up his business again, she'd be the first person that he sold off.

"She's been nothing but a pain in my ass since she was born. Christ, the way she used to follow me around like I was something special to her." Anna asked if he wondered if he was special to her. "Sure I was. I mean, who wouldn't want to be friends with me and shit like that? But she'd tell on me, how much I was drinking or smoking. Then she convinced our mother to keep track of all the money that she'd lent me. Who does that shit to their own big brother? Anyway, I was going to auction her off to the highest bidder. She owed me, anyway."

"What did you think she owed you?" He told her. "So, to you simply being born made her owe you something. I don't know how that was supposed to be her fault, but that's not a question, now is it? This money that you got off your mother, why didn't you pay her back? I mean, you did say you would, yet you didn't even bother."

"Why should I have to pay back my own mom for money that she had in excess? She had me—there wasn't any reason that she should stop taking care of my needs just because

I'm a grown man. No, I told her that because that's what she wanted to hear. We both knew that I had no intentions of paying her back." Anna asked him if he knew how much that money had come to. "I don't know. I don't think it was as much as Meggie was put out about. What? A couple of grand or so? I don't even care anymore. Now that we're going to get things taken care of, I'll not bother her again about it. But I will need cash."

Anna punched him in the face. While he was down and bleeding, she kicked him in the ribs, over and over until he was sure that she'd managed to break every one of them. There was no fighting her back either. Christ, she was quick and mean. When she seemed to be stopping, she reached into his pants and took out his wallet.

"What the hell are you doing? That has nothing to do with anything we've talked about here. When I get up from here, Anna, you had better be prepared for the beating of your life. I'm not kidding you." She took out two one hundred dollar bills he had and tossed the rest, with his wallet, onto the table. "I want that back. If you even think about taking that to Meggie, I'm going to sue you."

Standing up was a good deal harder than he thought it should have been. Before he could get on his feet from his knees, Anna read him his rights. Rogen then asked him if he understood them as they'd been read to him.

"What's this about? You said that I'd be taken care of." The men with them jerked him from the floor, then handcuffed him. Both his wrists as well as his legs. "What the fuck do you think you're doing?"

"Arresting you, moron. What did you think was going to happen after we brought you in here?" He asked about his

125

needs being taken care of. "They will be. In prison. Where you will be spending the rest of your life."

As soon as the family left him there, the men gathered around him. No matter how many times he tried to tell them that this was not right, that it was unfair of them, they continued as if he'd not said a word. Shoved into the back of an awaiting van, he saw a man sitting there.

"This is going to get someone killed." The man mumbled something, but Jake didn't understand what he said. "I'm not going to go to prison. I'm not even going to jail."

"You're right about that." As soon as the door closed to the van, the man stood up. It was someone that looked like a person he knew. Then it hit him. Shane Picket. "You've fucked with my family for far too long. Taken what didn't belong to you in the way of my pack. Sold them to people who used them then killed them. Goodbye, Jake."

He felt Shane wrap his arms around his throat. They were powerful, and much bigger than he thought the man would have been. The air wasn't cut off as he thought it might be, but then he felt the quick movement of his head.

Chapter 9

Morgan didn't feel the least bit bad for what he'd done to Jake Simons. He'd meant to sell off their mother. Profit off her being raped and killed. It was what he'd done to other cats that he'd taken. Shifters too. Jake would know exactly what was done to them, because the person that purchased the shifter would send him videos of it. They had come across them when they'd come out here last night while going through his house.

"How are you doing now?" Morgan looked at Anna, who was nursing a busted knuckle, when she spoke. "I'm doing wonderfully. You should be as well."

"I am. Honestly. I don't know who killed the man, but I have to say that I'm glad for it. He would have continued to prosper in prison. Rogen told me that after she found out that one of his people was running part of his ring from the prison walls out there. He would have done the same thing." Anna nodded and sat down on his lap. "Rogen said all she was going to tell Mom was that he died on the way to jail. That's all she needs to know. I figure after she finds out what sorts of things he was doing out there, Mom would have washed her hands of him anyway."

"Did I tell you that I took the money to her yesterday? She, of course, didn't want it. I suggested that she use the money to buy some beautiful flowers to put on her parents' graves. Meggie said that she'd do that." Morgan held Anna to him. "I've hired a nanny. Two of them, as a matter of fact. Rogen wants me to come and work for her. I told her that I'd think about it."

"What is holding you back from telling her that you will?" Anna said she didn't know if she could work with Rogen. Morgan laughed. "I don't know how anyone would be able to work for Rogen, but she does do a great job."

"She does. How she can remember how to do that on all those different computers is well beyond me. But she loves it. She wants me to work with her because I'm good at hand to hand combat. I don't have any formal training, but I have a great deal of street smarts that she said she doesn't. Rogen is all black and white. I'm more of a gray area kind of thinker." Morgan asked her what else they needed for Williams and the prison. "Nothing. We won't have to be there, of course. The more we stay out of something like that, the less likely someone will figure out what she does here. I'm all for keeping out of it anyway. That's some scary shit going down."

It was too. They were going to arrest Parker Williams and every person that worked at the prison. Even the custodial staff was in on getting the convicts out of the place. Just yesterday Rogen had figured out that they were slipping people into the place too. It was a safe haven for them to hide in. No one would suspect a criminal to be hidden inside the prison to keep from being arrested.

"I'd like to propose something to you. You can say no if you'd like, but I was thinking that we need to start getting ready for the holidays." She turned on his lap and looked at him. "Hear me out. In order to do this holiday up nice, I think that we'll have to spend a week or two in New York, then a couple more weeks in Paris. With the kids."

"The nannies will have to travel with us as well." He nodded and said that he thought they'd have to. "Why so early? Do you know something that I don't?"

"I'm certain that I don't, but I need to get away before classes begin again. My entire office is being renovated right now. Not to mention, there are all kinds of things that I have to deal with there before we leave. I need to make sure that no one knew what Long was up to before he hurt you." She asked if he was sure of it yet. "Yes. I am. I hate that. We've had so much going on here that it's hard to believe that anything else could go wrong, but I'd—"

"Nothing has really gone wrong, Morgan. I mean, we have three beautiful children. Jake is no longer a threat to your mom. By the way, did you know that he'd been threatening her for a long time?" Morgan told her that he'd not known any of that. "I didn't think you did or you would have done something sooner. Back to my list. You've been promoted. I found you. You found me. We have a nice home, and we're in love."

"All good things, I assure you. But once this gets out about Long, if they find evidence that Bart and the others knew about it, it's going to be a shit storm. They're going to start looking at grades, the other professors, as well as every student that has left the university. They'll also want to know the reasons why they left." Anna said she'd not thought of that. "I hadn't either, but Dad came by to run it by me. He's even the one that suggested we get away for a few weeks so we can't be caught up in it."

"So when does this take place? I'm assuming that you have that planned out already, and were just waiting on this thing with the prison to be taken care of." He told her when his meeting was. "At six this evening. I guess that getting it over with sooner rather than later is better. Are you taking anyone with you?"

"No. I need to get this taken care of on my own. I have a feeling that I might not be dean when I return either. I'm sort of hoping so." Anna asked him why. "I don't know, really. I wanted the job, dreamed of having it. But with you and the kids, I think that I'd rather have something a little more settled. This job won't be when this is all taken care of. It's doubtful if it will be again."

"I want you to know that I will be behind you every single step of the way. Also, I'll be beside you if they decide to can your pansy ass." Morgan kissed her on the nose. "You do know that I love you, Morgan. Don't you?"

"I do. That, right now, is the only thing that I'm sure of. That, and that I love our kids too." He stood up, setting her on her feet when he did. "I'm going to head over there now and see what I can find out about other things. I might need you something terrible when I return."

"You will always have me. Forever and a day." He didn't know how much he'd needed to hear that until she said it. Getting in his car, he was nearly to the university when he realized this might be his last time coming here.

Morgan had been a teacher since he'd graduated from

college. First he'd started out as an elementary teacher, then moved his way up the ladder to where he was now. Taking the job was what he thought he wanted. Now he only wanted to be at home, work when he had to, and be a good father and husband to his family.

There was only his and one other car in the parking lot when he pulled in. The meeting was in another thirty minutes, so he wondered where they were. Almost as soon as he had the thought, several cars pulled in at once and they got out of their cars. He could smell the alcohol on each one of them, as well as the fact that a couple of them had smoked some weed. Two things that were against the rules that had been outlined to him by them.

As they entered the big building, he wished now that he'd taken up his brother's offer of coming with him. At the very least he wished that Rogen had come. She'd found all the paperwork that was necessary for this to get finished up. The president of the college, David Kildare, was in the room when they entered. So was Rogen.

Since he'd been the one that wanted the meeting, he wasn't sure where to go. When Rogen asked everyone to sit down, he did as well. Her winking at him had him thinking that he was just going to be one of the guys when President Kildare stood up and cleared his throat.

"I wasn't aware of all the facts on the Long case until I was contacted by not just the board of directors, but also the FBI. I was confused about that until they sat me down and explained to me just what had been going. Right under my nose." The doors opened again and two FBI agents walked in, one of whom he knew. Agent Patrick Donaldson sat down in the chair next to him. "First of all, I'd like to thank Professor

Morgan Robinson for saving the life of one of our students. Without his help and quick actions, there is no telling how much longer this might have gone on."

Patrick stood up. "As of the day that Mr. Long was killed, we began an investigation into how this could have happened. We started looking at his roster, as well as some notes that we found in his desk. There were also things that I'm not going to name just yet, but suffice it to say, this college is going to be thoroughly investigated from the top to the bottom."

"Why wasn't I made aware of this?" Dean Sheppard stood up when Patrick sat down. "As head of deans in this building, I should have been made aware of their every move. I don't like being in the dark about this sort of thing."

"Sit your ass down." He watched as Sheppard sat down when Rogen told him to. "What do you mean you don't like being in the dark, Mr. Sheppard?"

"I'm Dean Sheppard to you. I don't know who you are, but you will have respect for me. I've worked very hard to get to where I am, and I won't have you disrespecting me by acting like this toward me and my fellow deans." If he expected the others to agree with him, Sheppard was sorely disappointed. "We've all worked very hard to get where we are."

"Sure you have. On the backs of others in your little man club." Rogen was on a roll, and Morgan had to fight hard not to laugh. "You were Paul Long's best friend, correct? You hung out at titty bars together. He even accompanied you to a few of your kind of bars, did he not? I don't know if you're aware of this or not, but no one gives a fuck that you're gay, Rick. I'm reasonably sure that they all knew it anyway."

Nodding heads confirmed what Rogen was saying. It had

never matter to Morgan what a person sexual preference was. He'd not known about Rick because he simply didn't care.

"I don't know what you're talking about." Rogen slid a file to Sheppard, and he opened it and closed it just as quickly. "This means nothing."

"No, that's what I was just saying. However, the few times that you were made aware of what sort of person Paul was, that is what everyone is going to be pissed off at you about." Rick stood up. "Sit the fuck down right now, or so help me, I'm going to have the agents here shoot you where you stand. Sit down."

He did. Hard too. Morgan was no longer trying not to grin, but he did hold in his laughter. When Rick looked directly at him, Morgan couldn't help it, he laughed a little. Whatever Rogen was going to do, he'd be happy as hell for it to be on her shoulders and not his. He might even be able to keep his job after this.

"What I'd like to talk to you about is the complaints that were sent to you by two hundred and forty-seven female students. This was about the behavior of Paul Long and how he'd raped them." Again, he denied knowing anything about it. "That is not what we found when we got into your computer this morning. There are over three hundred complaints about not just Long, but also Professor Jack Damion, now deceased. The written complaints about him aren't nearly the same as the ones about Long, but they were never addressed."

"You have no idea what you're talking about. Those complaints were filed with the bursar's office, and were to be sent to President Kildare. It's not my fault that they were lost on the way to him." Rogen pointed out that they were never sent to the bursar's office because they were still in a file on his computer. "Who the hell are you that you think you have the right to go through my things like you have? I demand that she tossed out of here and we get to the real meat of this meeting—raises."

"She has every right to do this because she works for the United States Government. Agent Rogan Robinson is married to Professor Morgan Robinson's brother. If not for Morgan, none of this would have ever come to light until someone got wind of it and it hit the papers." Patrick stood up and began to read Rick's rights to him. He asked what he was being arrested for. "There is a long list of things, but we're going to put right here on top that you were assisting Professor Long with the rape and sometimes murder of students that were supposed to be protected by you."

As soon as he was taken away, the meeting continued on the vein it was on with Rick. Morgan sat there as nearly half the men left in the room were arrested for their part in what Rick had been doing since he'd been made dean twelve years ago. The few that were left, including him, looked as nervous as he felt.

"As of this morning, the university has been closed down under the guise of having buildings updated, as well as some of the older buildings that are too far gone for us to repair being taken down. There will be programs open for people to come in and use the facilities, such as the pool and daycare centers. Those buildings will be watched carefully. After that—in about a year, I'm told—we'll open up under new management, including my job. And there will be a tighter crackdown on the teachers that will be kept on to work here." One of the professors that Morgan didn't know well asked what they were going to be doing. "That will be up to the new president. I will tell you this—before you leave here today, you will sign the nondisclosure paperwork again. If one word of what happened here gets to the press or any of the social media pages, this young woman here will hunt you down and make you regret every single letter that you printed. I'd take that to the bank if I were you too. She's a ball buster. Morgan, if you have a moment, I'd like to have a word or two with you."

"Yes sir."

He had no idea why he was being singled out, but he only just then realized that if they could keep this out of the paper, he'd not have to leave the country. However, he was going to anyway, just to be with his family. Morgan followed President Kildare and Rogen into his office. He didn't know what Anna was going to do about college now. But she could always take classes online, he thought.

~*~

Rogen watched Morgan. He was a good man, and she was glad that she'd been asked to help him out with this. When she'd been approached by Patrick as to what they were going to do, she'd been all for it. Anything to get this shit taken care of before anyone got wind of it. She didn't think, however, it was going to go the way that President Kildare thought it would.

They were all seated in the large office. Drinks were provided, as well as food on a large tray. Rogen had already eaten a bagel with cream cheese, and now she wanted one of the cherry filled Danish. She eyed it several times before she thought *fuck it* and took it off the tray. She was stressed out.

"I don't want it." The Danish was nearly to her mouth when Morgan spoke. "I have a feeling that you're going to

135

ask me to take over your job. I don't want it. In fact, I was seriously thinking that I'd like to be a stay at home dad."

"What do you mean, you don't want it? Damn it, boy, you've got to take it. A great many people are going to need someone like you running this ship." Morgan said that there were people out there who were more qualified for it than he was. "Perhaps they might be, but you have the guts and the heart to do a wonderful job here. Not only will you make this campus great again, but you'll be able to get anything you want with this little girl on your side."

"I just got married. I have three wonderful children. My brother and his wife, Rogen here, have a son that I'd really like to have fun with too. My mom and dad aren't getting any younger, and I want to spend as much time with them as humanly possible. This job, it was everything that I ever wanted in a place to claim as my own. Even your job would have been a great feather in my cap. But I've only just decided that I'm not cut out for being behind a desk all day, away from my family." Patrick laughed and handed Rogen a five dollar bill. "What's that all about?"

"I told him that you'd not want it. Bet him five bucks that you'd not just turn down the job, but that you'd quit the one you have before the end of the day." Morgan asked her how she knew. "The way you look at Anna when she's in the room. The fun you have with Eddie even though he's so young yet. The girls worship you. You were made to be a college professor, if you'd never met and fallen in love with Anna. I told you, Morgan, you're a good man."

"I don't know if in a few years I might want to come back, but for now, I'm not going to even think about this job. My family and I are going on a very long trip. Made longer now because of this decision." Morgan stood up and put out his hand. "Thank you for the opportunity to have been here for as long as I have. And more importantly, I thank you very much for the offer that I see I must turn down."

Rogen watched Morgan leave the office. He would be rethinking what he'd done today. Rogen had no doubt that before she could clean up the rest of the mess here he'd be thinking of getting his job back. She'd told Thatcher before she left what was going to happen here, and the things that she thought were going to be coming from Morgan. He had agreed with her one hundred percent.

It took her two hours to get things lined up at the university. The construction crew was going to come to the campus in the morning and begin work on this building first. There were just too many bad vibes coming from this one to not have it broken down and rebuilt. She thought that many of the students would like that very much.

"Thank you for letting me retire, Rogen. I don't know what I would have done if you had just let them take me away with the rest of them." Rogen told Kildare that he'd not been aware of any of it. There was no point in making him suffer because he had a bunch of idiots working for him. "Still, I should have been a little more on the ball, and perhaps I might have caught it sooner."

She didn't say anything to him. It would have ended sooner had he been a better president. His desk was being cleaned out even as they sat there. There was enough shit in this one room that she was sure his wife was going to pitch a bitch about all the clutter.

When she was alone in the building, Rogen looked around the offices. So many memories were here, she'd bet.

Not just bad ones, but very good ones too. Rogen had found out that this very building had been used for the graduation ceremonies for women when they'd gotten their degrees so very long ago. Women weren't meant to be smart, so they'd hidden away the ones that were.

Tomorrow morning she was going to go to the prison, where the men there were going to be arrested. No one had gotten wind of it simply because she had good people working with her. It wasn't her job to go out on these sort of things—she was the behind the scenes kind of person. But she wanted to be there when everyone was arrested. Rogen had her own special job to do.

Rogen was going to tell the Hayes men that they were now having the robbery of several banks added to their sentencing. That would mean that none of them would be released in her lifetime. The only way they were leaving there would be in a body bag. She hoped that it would be as soon as they were all in the general population together. They'd not take it well that Junior had fucked them over—or that he'd planned to.

When she got home that night, Thatcher met her at the door. He had Jimmy in his arms, and she took him after getting a kiss from her mate. Sitting in the living room, she held their son as she told him about the college, then what was going to happen as soon as it closed down.

"Mom is aware of Morgan quitting his job." Rogen asked him how she'd taken it. "Believe it or not, I think her and Dad were kind of glad that he was done. I know that Dad is working up some kind of plan to get Morgan to go into business with him. Whatever that is, they'll have fun at it."

"Your dad needs a hobby before your mom murders him. Did she tell you what he did yesterday? He got into the jelly

138

that she was planning on taking to the women's shelter, and opened about five jars of it for his buddies. I thought she was going to kill him. But he sat her down, gave her a dozen roses, and handed her a thick slice of bread with her marmalade on it. I guess it's her favorite." Thatcher said that it was. "You were called out early this morning. Is everything all right at work?"

"Yes. I was asked to help out with jobs that would take me away from here. To be a specialist in my field. I turned them down for that as well. I'm going to hang out my shingle with Dawson, and we're going to be country doctors together. I think we'll be good at it." She said that she thought they would as well. "What about you? You're not quitting your job, are you? That would be a tragedy of major proportions. Oh, you got a letter from your mom and Jamie today."

She was excited to hear from him as well. Reading the letter twice, she handed it to Thatcher. He and mom were getting to know each other again and having the time of their life. Rogen spoke to Jimmy as she changed his diaper.

"When Uncle Jamie gets back, he said that he's going to show you all the pictures that he's taken. Also, he told me to tell you that he loves you very much. So does Grandma Lisha." Rogen picked Jimmy up and gave him the hugs that were mentioned in the letter. "How about you and me veg out in front of the television and eat something bad for us? Well, I'll eat the bad stuff, and you will have a nice warm bottle."

Sitting on the couch with her little man, she thought about her day. It seemed to always be bad news anymore. Not just with the people around her, but with places that she had hoped would be violence free. Such as what she was going to do in the morning and what she'd done tonight.

While searching for a movie that would lull the little man to sleep, she told him what she'd been thinking. Rogen knew that she was going to have to stop that soon. Once he could understand her, she might crush his views on the world in general. Rogen was happy when Thatcher joined them with two glasses of tea to go with their movies.

"I hope that someday soon I can feel good about letting the kids out in the back yard without them getting shot or something." Thatcher asked her what had brought that on. "I don't know. It's been a really shitty week so far. How was your week? Anything good to report and bring me out of this sucky mood?"

"Let me think a moment. I delivered two children this week. I was helping out in ER on an emergency when one of the moms came in. The second baby was delivered in the parking lot when the dad pulled into the circle and passed out. He nearly made it." Rogen laughed when he did. "Also, I've given my notice, as I told you I was, and Dawson and I bought us a building together to have outfitted for a doctor's office. We've also decided to give one day a week to the hospital to help out when they have people on vacation."

"You said one day a week. Do you think they'll only let you do that?" He said not easily, but they would have to in the end. "Good. I think I'll like having you here more. You'll certainly be closer to home this way."

"You just want me nearby so you can order me around and jump my bones while you're at it." Rogen pretend to think about that and nodded. "How about when little man goes to sleep, we sneak upstairs and you can order me around all you want?"

"Deal. But you should really stop calling him little man,

don't you think? I mean, he might be as tall as you are, and that wouldn't set well with him." Thatcher pointed out that she was the one that had started calling him that. "Oh, I'm not going to stop calling him that. He will enjoy his mom calling him little man, or I'll show him the backside of my hand."

"Sure you will, honey. Sure you will." Bastard. She was going to really order him around now. He would do it too, because she was meaner than him. "I don't know what you're plotting, but I do love you."

"And I love you, Thatcher. Very much so."

Chapter 10

Noah was brought into a large room with no tables, four chairs that were bolted to the floor, as well as a thick loop that he'd bet anything he was going to be chained to. There was no reason to treat him like this, he thought. He'd only dug up the money from a long time ago. They'd been tried for that and found guilty already.

His father was brought in next. Dad had a black eye, as well as several stitches in his cheek. He wondered what the other guy looked like when he remembered how his dad had gotten beaten up. Someone had told Noah that he'd gotten the snot beat out of him when he wouldn't sit down when they told him that his other son was there.

Smiling about that, Noah waited until he was bolted to the floor before speaking. His dad had missed him, he thought. That was such a good thing to know. However, both his brothers were brought in just as he was getting ready to tease his father.

David was sitting next to him. He looked a little worse for

wear. Both his eyes were blackened, his upper and lower lip were sewed up, and he had a limp. When a cop had to take you down, it was a good bet you'd have a few things wrong with you.

Bud was sitting in his chair but not looking around—but then, he'd always been like that. Quiet as a church cat until he was prodded. Noah loved poking at his brother until he got so pissy that he'd leap at him. He couldn't do no more than just hit you a couple of times before he'd go back to sitting still with his head down.

The woman that came in was one he'd seen before. She'd been around town when he'd been looking for his sister. Anna never did have the sense that God gave her. Noah thought that she'd hang out with anybody, even dykes like this broad was.

"My name is Rogen Robinson. I'm an agent for the government." Dad asked her which branch. "All of them. I'm a special agent in charge of more shit than you could put names to. Now, shut the fuck up and listen to what I have to say. Thanks to dumbass here, Noah Junior, you're all going to be charged with the bank robberies of twelve different banks. We thought that you'd only been in—"

"Wait a damned minute here. I know the law better than you do, bitch, and you can't be trying us for the same crime two times. That's not fair." Noah was pretty proud of himself until she kicked him in the head, and his chair tilted back enough that his arms felt like they were being pulled out. "I'm gonna fall, bitch. Help me."

"As I was saying, thanks to numb nuts here, we're going to be able to charge you with each of the robberies that you committed over the course of ten years." She finally helped him back to the floor. Then she smacked him upside the head before talking again. "With the help of Anna's husband, and working with the federal government, Noah Junior here led him right to the place where you stored all the money from each of the robberies. Good job."

"Wait. Wait a fucking second here. Are you telling me that my own son gave us up? You saying that he was the one that is getting us all more sentences?" Noah looked at his dad when he said his name. "You'd better be watching your back, son. I'd sure hate to have something happen to you."

"Did you just threaten me? Did you hear that, bitch? He just threatened me. What you gonna do about that." Noah watched her while she thought about it. Waiting for an answer from her, his dad started laughing. "Do you hear him? He's gonna do it. He's gonna have me kilt."

"Sorry, not sorry. I didn't hear a fucking thing. In actuality, I don't care what happens to any of you. I do know that Anna and her husband are going to feel much better about raising their children in a world without you four in it." Dad asked about Anna having kids. "She has three. Twin little girls and a son."

"No, that can't be right. Her's a tiger." David looked at dad when he didn't understand. "Her can't have kids. You said that you'd fix it so she'd not have any more monsters like her. No. No way. She have monsters?"

"No. She has kids that will grow up knowing that they're being loved and well cared for." Dad looked at him, then back at Rogen. "You have something to ask me, Noah Senior?"

"She wasn't mine. I'm guessing you know that." Rogen nodded. "She never did want to be a part of my family. Never wanted to have fun with us. She was too uppity for it. Now she's got herself some brats that'll be just like her."

"I hope so." Dad just shook his head. "She'll never come to see any of you. I'd not expect to see her children either. She's happy now. In love and loved. Not that you care, but I thought that you'd like to know that despite having you as her parent, she's done well with her life."

"You're right. I don't give a shit what happens to her. If'n I had my way, she'd of been dead a long time ago. My wife, she never should have taken that thing into my house. That weren't right of her." Rogen asked him if he'd killed her over it. "Since they can't give me life more'n once, I'll tell you that I did. Ruth was a good woman when she wanted to be. Gave me these here boys. They're a might messed up, but I blame that on her too. She should have taken care to behave herself so I'd not knock her around when she was having one of them."

"So, your wife does a good deed and you kill her over it." Dad said it weren't go good deed to him. "No, I suppose only you would think the world only revolves around you. Look at your children, Noah. Bud can barely look at anyone because of what you did to him. David has several disabilities that keeps him from learning the basics of everyday life. Then here is Junior. Stupider than the other two simply because he knows better, but just doesn't give a shit about anyone but himself. You did a stellar job raising these three. You should be proud of yourself. All four of you under the same roof in a fucking prison, because you never gave a fuck about how your actions would harm someone else."

"You damned right I didn't. You want to know why? Because if you don't be man enough to take what you want, then you won't amount to a hill of beans." Noah was so proud of his dad in that moment that he would have been willing to take a cuff to the head just to hug him. "You want to know what else there, missy? I shouldn't be arrested for having the smarts enough to take care of my family when they needed it. I'm a man of honor."

"You're a man without worth at all, you moronic fuck. You stole money that didn't belong to you. You murdered when someone got into your way, and you raised your sons to be exactly like you." Dad sat up straighter in his chair, and so did he. "That wasn't meant to boost your already over inflated ego. You're a fucking terror to this world, and had I been your wife, I would have murdered you in your sleep the first time you touched me with your fist. You, you son of a bitch, are nothing. Not to me or to Anna. And while I know that means shit to you, I hope you rot in Hell."

"She wasn't hurting nobody." They all looked at Bud as he rocked back and forth. "Momma was just hanging out the laundry because the dryer was busted, and he came up behind her and hit her in the head with a frying pan. I wouldn't eat no more chicken after that."

"Bud, did you see your father hit your mother?" He didn't answer Rogen, but continued to rock back and forth as he kept talking. "Bud, what else do you know about your family?"

"Killed my friend when we were little. Junior just strangled him to death on account 'a him being a black person. My momma, she said that the N word ain't nice, and I wasn't to call people that no matter what. I had to when they was around, but I didn't mean it. Killed him by strangling the life right out of him, when he was my friend." Noah stared to speak, but the look that Rogen gave him had his balls tighten up around him. "I tried to be good for my momma, but they hurt me all the time. I have no balls because Daddy said that I was too stupid to breed. I never did nothing to no girl, but now I got nothing at all. He just cut them off me when I was tied to the bed."

Rogen called for help and three men came rushing in. "Are you recording this?" They all nodded that they were. "Write down what he says too. I don't want to miss a thing."

"David and I were good boys, Momma told me. But Daddy, he beat us all the time when we just wanted to stay home with Momma. She would make us fried pies when they was gone." Noah was pissed about that. He never got any pies. "She loved us. She told us that all the time. Momma loves her little Bud and David."

"She never did that. How come when I asked for pies she told me that she didn't have the stuff to make it? That ain't right. No way." Rogen wasn't paying any attention to him, so he kicked out at her. "Did you hear me? That ain't right. I wanted some fried pies too."

"Shut the fuck up before I rip your fucking face off." He had a feeling that she wasn't kidding either. So he sat there listening to his brother while he told her everything that they had done to him and David. "Bud, can you tell me, if you know, where the other people are buried? I'd like to tell their parents where they are."

Her voice was like his momma's when she talked to Bud. Like she was the sweetest thing in the world, when he knew better. Making fried pies for the other two was about the worsterest thing she could have done. Not making him any when he was the oldest was just not right in his book.

Bud went on and on about things for so long that Noah

just wanted to tell him to shut up. Since his daddy wasn't having any luck with getting Bud to shut his trapper, then he knew he wouldn't either. It was like Bud had scribbled things down and was just now reading them off. Which was just stupid, because he couldn't read or write.

Then his brother looked right at him. It was the scariest thing he'd ever seen. Even the dyke had never looked at him like Bud was looking at him. When he didn't say anything for some time, Noah looked around the room.

"What's up his ass?" Bud leaped at him as if he had super strength. Like one of them superhero's that he loved to watch on television. He was chained up like he was, sure. But the chains groaned, like they were just barely holding him back. "Bud, whatcha thinking about?"

"Killing you." The hair on his arms and the back of his neck tingled, just like when he got a balloon and rubbed it on his body. "I'm gonna kill you, Junior. You watch and see. Just snap your neck like you're nothing but a turtle."

Not only did he not know what to say to that, Noah couldn't even think of a good comeback. He had a feeling that Bud would do just what he said. Just walk up to him, snap his neck like a turtle, then walk away.

"I want some protection." Rogen just stood up and moved to the door when Bud finally stopped talking. "Did you hear me? I want something to protect me. First my daddy said he was gonna kill me, now my own brother is. What is this world a coming to?"

"I could care less if they both were in on killing you, then left your body out for the buzzards to pick over." Dad was taken out of the room while she stood there smiling at him. "I have a feeling, Junior, that you're not going to last till the end

149

of the week. That's not really anything that I'll lose sleep over, but then I doubt anyone will."

It was just him and Bud in the room when they took David away. He was talking about fried pies and could he please have one. When the door shut behind them, leaving just him, Bud, and an officer, Noah asked again if he could have someone watching over him. Of course he was told to shut his mouth.

Bud was next to go back to his room. When he stood up, he asked the officer that was holding onto his chains if he could stretch out real big. Given permission, Noah watched his little brother push his arms way up over his head. There was muscle there, not fat like Noah had on his belly. And Bud's arms looked like giant logs they were so built up. He wanted to look like that too, and asked his brother how he'd gotten so buffed up.

It happened so quickly that Noah wasn't sure his brother was loose until the chains were wrapped up tight around his neck. He was thinking of shiny ribbons when he saw that the officer was trying to get Bud to let him breathe. Bud wasn't letting go for nothing. As the room started to darken up a bit, Noah knew that his brother was going to kill him. When he couldn't lift up his arms to try to pull the chains away no more, he just closed his eyes. Bud had killed him sure as shit.

~*~

Anna didn't move from the couch when she heard the phone ringing in another part of the house. Renee was sleeping on the blanket that she'd laid out for her and Marie. Marie was trying her best to pull herself along in her super crawl, as Morgan called it. Eddie was sleeping on her chest, just finishing his bottle. Anna looked at the doorway when

Morgan entered the room.

"Rogen called to see if you were all right." Morgan sat down on the chair next to her and picked up Marie when she called him da-da. "I don't think that I'll ever get over hearing that. Are you all right?"

"For now, yes." Eddie stretched and she smiled at him. "They're dead. All three of them are dead. I mean, I figured that eventually they'd be killed, especially Junior. But to have had Bud kill Junior was nothing that I expected at all."

"I can't imagine the strength it took for Bud to have been able to kill Junior when there were nine officers beating on him to stop. But I guess the blows to his head and body were too much for him, and he died. Poor guy. He'd been treated so badly, don't you think?" She nodded. "Bud and David both were a product of their upbringing. They all three were, but those two suffered the most, I think."

"Rogen said that when she went back to check on David after it was determined that Bud and Junior were both dead, David had killed himself by hanging. I guess he'd been told just moments before, and knew that he couldn't live without Bud. They protected each other a great deal." Morgan asked her if she knew about Noah Senior. "Is he dead as well?"

"No. But he has been put on suicide watch until they can get him someplace that he'll be safe. The only thing he was upset about was that he'd not been able to kill Junior himself. That's a hell of a family, right there." Anna nodded and burped Eddie. "Anna, I'd still like to take us away for a little while. Are you still wanting to go?"

"Yes. But not right now. In a couple of days. Do you know what will happen to the bodies?" He said that he could find out. "I've decided that I want to bury Bud and David someplace nice. Junior can be buried in the prison yard for all I care about him. I think he was the one that made the other two suffer the most."

"I think you're right." She nodded. Anna felt rung out. "I'm going to take the girls outside now that Marie is awake, and show them the back yard. They love to watch the trees sway. You rest here. All right?" Thanking him, she didn't move even when he kissed her on the cheek.

It wasn't as if she was going to miss them—not any of them. But to have lost three people that she'd grown up with in a matter of an hour was just too much. David she remembered as being so kind when Junior or Noah Senior weren't around. He would pick flowers for Ruth, and she'd make a big show of him bringing her mostly weeds to make the house prettier.

Bud had been an old soul even when he'd been little. He only had the one friend when he'd been growing up, and now she knew what had happened to the youngster. Rogen was bringing in dogs, she told her, to see if she could find his body, along with the other four that he'd mentioned. All people that hadn't been like them, so they'd murdered them.

Meggie joined her a little while later, just as she was dozing off. She said she'd come back later, but Anna said that she needed to get up anyway. That the girls were out with their dad in the yard.

"I've come to talk to you, honey. I need your help." Anna would do anything for Meggie, but today her heart wasn't in it. "You can do this. I'm sure of it. There is a huge auction going on down the road tomorrow. I wanted to go since I first heard about it, but Thatch, he hates those kind of things. He just doesn't care for the uncertainty of them. Also, not getting things for the price he wants. Anyway, I thought you, me, and Rogen could go. It'll be an all-day event, but a great deal of fun."

"I've never been to an auction before. I wouldn't know the first thing about them." Meggie actually clapped her hands. "I would think that is a bad thing."

"Oh, it is if you don't have an expert with you. That's why you're lucky to have me going with you. Rogan hasn't ever been to one either. Not when she wasn't looking for someone to capture or kill, anyway. That girl scares me a little." Anna told her that everyone was afraid of Rogen, including Meggie's sons. "Really? Good. That's the way it should be, I think."

"What's at this auction that you're hoping to get?" Meggie said there was nothing specific, and that was the point. "Okay. I'm not sure that's a good answer, but sure, I'll go with you. Did I tell you that Morgan is going to be a home dad? I'm going to be working with Rogen."

"Yes, he did tell me that. And I'm very proud of him. I think he really enjoyed the idea of teaching college, just not the actual teaching part. This will be good for you both. So long as I can watch the children too." Anna told her again that she didn't have to have a reason to want them to be with her, just to come and get them. "I'll get that way soon, but right now I know that you and Morgan are enjoying having so much fun with them. Besides, I want to get to know you a lot more before I go taking your children away for the night. I can do that, can't I?"

"Of course. I think they'll enjoy that as much as you will." Meggie asked her if she would have rules about them coming over. "Rules? I don't know what you mean. If you mean that you can't feed them something that they don't get here, then

I'd be all right with them having that special relationship with you. So long as you don't overdo it, or do something that is complete out of the question to us."

"I would never override anything that you have laid down the law about. You can count on that. But I was thinking more like bedtimes and snacks in bed sort of rules." Anna laughed and told her no, that she was fine with them spending time with their grandma on her terms. "I thank you for that. I cannot wait to take them shopping with me. Trips to the zoo. I know that they're much too young for that now, but I have to tell you, we're making plans, Thatch and I."

"About this auction." Meggie said she'd forgotten all about it. "You really want me to come with you? As I said, I know nothing about them."

"You'll do fine so long as you follow these rules. Don't take the first bid that is out there. Never tell anyone but who you're with what you're bidding on. Set you a price you want to pay for something, and stick to it. And my favorite is for you to enjoy yourself. All the people there can go to Hades for all I care if I get something they wanted. That is the best fun I've ever had." Anna saw a side of Meggie that she'd never seen before, and she loved it. "I'll pick you up in the morning. It starts at ten, but I like to get there early to scope things out a little bit. The things that I like to get are the box lots. They have so much more junk in them than treasure, but it's fun picking through it."

Morgan came in with the other two when Eddie was just waking up. He was staying awake longer and longer now, and Anna loved it. Meggie was so excited when both the girls wanted her to take them. As she sat on the floor with them, she pulled out books for them and sat there reading to all three of them.

"Dad wants me to hang out with him tomorrow. He told me that you ladies were going to an auction." Anna told him what his mom had told her. "You'll love it. Mom is really good at it. I'm a little worried about Rogen. She might get mad if someone dares to outbid her."

"I never thought of that. Maybe we should tell her not to take any weapons. That way we can at least be assured that she won't draw on someone in the crowd when they start to go higher than she does." They were all laughing when Thatch joined them. "I think we should have a nice cookout tonight. How about steaks on the grill? I think I overheard someone complaining about how we're not home much anymore."

The plans were set, and Morgan invited the rest of the family over. They were going to have fun tonight, and Anna promised herself that she wasn't going to think about anything other than the loved ones that she had with her today. As soon as Rogen and Thatcher joined them, they set Jimmy on the floor with Eddie and told them what they'd been up to.

"You have no idea of the paperwork that is involved in having someone work for me." She asked her if there was anything wrong with that. "No. But you'll be happy to know that you're as clean as a virgin on her first date."

"Rogen. Really." Rogen winked at her when Meggie scolded her. "My goodness girl, don't you ever say a word without cursing in some way or making a dirty remark?"

"No. And that is why you love me so much, Meggie my dear. I keep you on your toes." With a quick hug, the three of them went out on the deck, leaving the men to work around their cook. "I have some news for you. You're not going to like it. Morgan knows, but he said to talk to you about it."

"What is it? I've already decided that I'm not going to allow anything to bother me for the rest of the day. If you screw that up for me, I'm going to be really pissed at you." Meggie huffed, and said that their kids were going to curse before walking. "So long as they know that they're loved, I could care less."

"There is a reward for finding the money from the banks. It's quite a bit. I was wondering who we should make the checks out to." Anna asked her how much was quite a bit. "Over two million. There were thirteen different money bags with bank names on them. More bags than that, of course, but those are the different banks."

"I thought that there were only about fifteen bags in total." Rogen told her that when they searched Bud's room to clean it out, they'd found notes. "He knew where it all was. Do you suppose that he was going to use it someday?"

"No. We all believe that he figured he'd not last long in prison. He wasn't all that violent for the most part. Strong as an ox, but not one to fight back. Bud was targeted a great deal by men bigger than him. We think that he wrote it all down so that if anything ever did happen to him, then someone would be able to collect it back. There were other things that he had in a notebook." Anna asked if they were important. "Yes. If you'd like to read—"

"No. I wouldn't. I don't think I want to." Rogen nodded. "To be honest with you, I didn't think he could read or write. I wonder if David could."

"No, he couldn't. Would it have been possible that Ruth showed him how to do both? You should know that David shouldn't have been as advanced as he was either. I think that Ruth did a good job on both those boys. She must have been a hell of a woman." She was, Anna told her. "Okay, you think about it and I'll get back to you about it."

"I know." Rogen sat back down. "I want it used for the education of people with disabilities like my brothers."

"I like that. Yes, that's perfect." When she walked away, Anna got up to join the rest of the family. She was happier every day that she'd come here to get away from it all. And boy, did she ever get away from it all. Life was suddenly very good.

Chapter 11

Shasta hated to grocery shop, especially when she had to bring the kids. All they wanted to do was to fill her cart with things that were no good for them. Every time she made her way up to the cashier, she had to dump a great many things out before they were rang up. It was annoying as hell.

"You put that package of cookies in the cart once more, Sam, and I will beat you to death with it." People stopped and stared at her. She would never do that, of course, but people acted like she had already done it. "Mind your own business, please. I'm just trying my best to make sure that they eat a decent meal."

She was embarrassed, and hated that feeling. Telling Jacob to watch his brother, she put all the things in the little basket that she picked up each time she had to shop with the kids. It was nearly full when she looked up and saw her sister.

Tru's life was nothing that she'd ever want. While her kids drove her insane most of the time, her sister's life was empty. She had a job, Shasta knew, but she rarely if ever took any time off for herself. And she would never watch the kids for her because she was forever out of town. When Tru hugged the three of them, Shasta asked her what was going on.

"Nothing. I just figured you'd be here because it's the first of the month, and came to see what else you had planned for the day." Shasta said she didn't have anything going on. "And you call my life boring. I'm going out of town in the morning, and I wanted to come by and tell you. I've got someone watching the house, but I didn't want you to worry if you didn't see me for a few weeks."

"Tru, I rarely see you more than once a month as it is. While I'm happy that you told me that you were leaving, I probably wouldn't have noticed you were gone unless it was a couple of months before I saw you." Tru laughed. That was another thing about her sister. She never seemed to understand when someone was insulting her. "Are you taking that brute of a dog with you?"

"You know that I am. I don't go anywhere without Charlie." She tickled the kids and asked them if they were ready for school to start soon. "I bet you are. I loved school when I was there."

"You didn't go for that long, Tru, so it would be difficult for you to relate to most children about school for that reason." True shrugged, and Shasta noticed that she seemed to be looking around. "Is there someone else you're here to see? I thought that you'd come to see me."

"I did, and no, I'm not seeing anyone else here. We're leaving in the morning. I just came by to give you that information." Shasta thanked her, and when her sister left them, she realized that all the food that she'd tossed out in the little basket was back in her cart. She could hear her sister laughing as she made her way out of the store.

After taking twenty minutes to load all her things on the conveyor belt, taking out the food that she didn't want, Shasta was on her way home. The kids were yelling about having lunch out, and she was just exhausted enough to do it today. She could not wait until they were all back in school so she could have a minute's peace.

While she helped the kids with their meals — why were catsup packets so difficult to open? — she thought about what to have for dinner. Her husband wouldn't be home for dinner, and she thought about just ordering a pizza. But two meals that she hadn't cooked for her kids was too much, so she tried to think of the easiest thing she could put together. The lure of pizza kept coming back to her.

Trying to think of something else, her thoughts went back to her sister. Tru's real name was Trudy. Trudy Justice. Shasta had always thought that her choice of nickname was ridiculous, since her name became Tru Justice. But if it didn't bother her sister that much, she would keep her mouth shut about it. Grandma Jenny had named her that. And no one ever went against Grandma Jenny when she declared something to be finished.

Shasta had never been to her sister's home. She knew that it was a nice one on a nice street. But since she'd moved into it without consulting her about it first, Shasta had decided that she wasn't going to go there. It really wasn't that Tru *had* to consult her on such things, but it would have been nice since she was the older of the two of them. Getting the kids into the car, she thought that if more people would consult her on things, then they would be better. Like the Parent Teachers Association.

Shasta being the president for four years straight had made the school money. They had new playground equipment, as well as new uniforms for the little peewee football players. She'd been so proud of her accomplishments that she would only mention it a few times each meeting that she'd been the one who had worked the hardest to get them in the position they were in. Then at Monday's meeting, she'd been asked to step down.

"What? I don't understand why you'd even ask me to do something like that. No, I won't step down. I'm the only one that works this hard, and you know it." The principal told her that it was time to give someone else a shot at it. "So they can mess up all my hard work? No, I don't think so. I've made this the way it should have been years ago."

"Mrs. Arnold, you don't even have kids going to this school. Since your son was sent to private school we've allowed you to have an extra term. But it's time for you to retire your position here and allow someone else to take the job. Someone that has children here." She had asked him what that had to do with anything. "Because, as I have pointed out to you before, on several occasions, you must have a child in the school for you to be voted in. I don't even know how you got this last term, when I know for a fact that you were voted out."

"I simply won't have it, Principal Collins. I won't. And the reason that I'm still here is because everyone knows that I get the job done." He told her he was sorry, but she was to no longer show up at meetings or they would get her for trespassing. Like they were really going to do that.

Putting the groceries away was finished up and the boys were watching television. Shasta went out on the deck and looked around their back yard. She really wanted to do some improvements there, but Mike, her husband, had told her that she could have the yard or private school for Sam. She knew where her priorities were, and she opted for the school.

Shasta wanted a pool, with a nice pool house beside it. The single tree that graced their back yard was dying, and she hadn't known why until a few weeks ago, when she caught Sam showing Jacob how to pee on it. She had beat his bottom hard, then sent him to bed without his supper. Mike had thought it was the funniest thing ever, and had not only allowed Sam to have dinner with them, but he also gave him a high five about doing his business outside.

Mike was having an affair — she was almost positive about that. He no longer wanted to have sex with her, and that was the only reason that she could come up with. For a while she thought that he was having one with her sister. Tru told her that she didn't care all that much for Mike, and wouldn't have sex with him if he had a golden cock that had been blessed by a high priestess. Sometimes the things that spilled from her sister's mouth made her wonder if they were related at all.

Walking into the kitchen to figure out dinner, she was surprised to see the television on. While she didn't care for what the staff did while they were on their own time, when they were on hers, they'd better be paying attention to her and what she wanted finished up.

Before she could tell them to get back to work, the cook told her that she was so sorry. The tone and the way that she said it made Shasta think that she wasn't the least bit sorry for not working. Then she heard the name of her husband's firm mentioned on the television.

Turning it up to hear, she saw her husband of ten years

being escorted out of his building with his hands in cuffs, with his jacket over it. She might not have known it was him, but she'd just picked that tie out for him to wear today.

"...arrested in conjunction with a yearlong investigation of Mr. Arnold's business. He's been arrested for tax fraud and money laundering so far. There are other charges that were being listed, but this reporter, along with a great many others, was cut off when the FBI showed up." Shasta felt a chair hit her in the back of the knees. Sitting down, she listened to the woman reporter say each of the names of those that had been arrested so far.

She had no idea how long she sat there. The news droned on for hours, it seemed like. Each time they showed the front of the Justice Building, a building that her parents and grandparents had built, they would put up a picture of her husband. Mike, in his nice suit and freshly cut hair, looked so happy in his employee photo.

When someone knocked on the front door, she didn't even bother moving. Whoever it was, she didn't want to talk to them. Getting up when the person knocked harder, Shasta wiped her tears away and made her way to the door.

Slamming the door almost as soon as the microphone was shoved in her face, Shasta was able to lock it too. Looking out the peephole, as she should have done in the first place, she could not believe how many people where there.

There were news vans out there that she'd never heard of. Local ones too that were setting up their equipment all over her yard and the sidewalk beyond. She started to go out and tell them to get off her flowers when she realized that might be just what they wanted. For her to go outside so that they could find out what she knew.

Trying to call Mike, all she got was his voice mail. Shasta should have figured that they would have taken his phone away from him. But she wanted answers, and having to leave him a recording wasn't getting her anywhere.

When the door opened behind her, Shasta was pushed away and knocked to her knees. Her father came in, and did not look like he was happy. Neither, for that matter, did her mom.

"What the Sam Hill has that man done to my company? Do you have any idea how long and hard we had to work to make it the company it is...well, what it was before this? Good Christ, I'm going to kill him." Mom told Dad to hush, the kids could hear him. "I'm sure they're going to be hearing a lot more than a few cuss words when they go to school next. With this shit out there, Shasta darling, I'd not send them anywhere. Where is Tru?"

"I don't know. She came by today when I was out shopping, and told me she was going to be gone for a while. Where does she go?" Dad just turned his back to her and she looked at her Mom. "What does Tru do for a living that she can't be here in my hour of need? Do you know?"

"I haven't the foggiest. I'm sure that whatever it is, she's enjoying herself." Her parents had always been so proud of Tru, yet neither of them knew what she did for a living. She asked if Tru might be a hooker or something. "Don't be jealous, Shasta. Tru is a good girl, and whatever she's doing, you know that we're proud of her. We are you too, but you will remember that we told you not to marry Mike."

"What has he done to bring you down on him now?" Then Shasta remembered the news reporting. "That might not even be his fault—have either of you thought of that? I swear, why am I always having to defend him to you? He's a good man, and a great father."

"He's neither of those. And he is responsible for this mess. I told the FBI what he was doing months ago." Shasta looked at her dad when he spoke. "I knew what he was doing the moment you convinced me that he needed to have a job to make himself feel like he was part of the family. Well, look at what he's done to make himself a wonderful part of it. He's ruined my company."

"Dad, you told on him?" He said of course he had. "Why would you do that? Why didn't you just tell him to stop? This is going to ruin me for all my clubs, and the things that I'm in charge of around town."

"Shasta, you're only thinking of yourself again. That's not right." Shasta looked at her mom. "You know as well as I do that he's not been a good father. He's barely been a husband to you. We've been carrying your finances for the last year, did he tell you that?"

"No. Why would you have to do that?" Dad answered from the living room where the boys were. "What do you mean he invested our money badly? That's not possible. We have plenty of money. Why, I've been able to put Sam in private school, we're doing so well."

"We got him in that school to shut you up." Shasta looked at her mom again. "You were harping on us so much about it that it was either tell you what we knew, which we weren't supposed to do, or pay for it. He's going to have to drop out of that now. I'm not going to be paying for your bills and ours when you have a husband that is going to prison."

Shasta wanted them to go away and leave her alone. They were both saying mean and cruel things to her. When she asked them to leave her home, Dad said that she needed to know what was what. She asked him what he was talking about.

"Three months ago I noticed that the bank notes weren't covered. Nor was payroll. I hired me someone to have a look into it, and found that Mike was skimming money from all the accounts to cover the shit he was snorting up his nose. Not to mention the two women that he has set up in apartments around town. I thought about going to him about it, even tried to get in to see him, and was told that Mike didn't want to talk to me right now. So I made my way to the police. Then the Feds." Shasta asked again why no one had told her. "Because they didn't know, and neither did we, if you were helping him out. You have to admit, you've been spending money on things like you had it."

"I thought we did have it." She looked around her home and realized how much was new. She'd been spending money to try and make Mike stay at home with her. "He's having an affair too?"

"Yes. As far as I could find out, he's been having them since the day you married the ass hole."

The room started to fuzz in and out until she felt herself tilting out of her chair. It was too much. All this was just too much for her.

~*~

Huston never watched television while he was working. The music could be blasting away, but the television was a major distraction. Putting the next pot on the shelf beside him, he heard the stereo change to the next disc. Before he could wonder what was up next, the room was blasting with his favorite band, one that he'd seen in concert more times than he could remember.

Working on the next pot, he was startled when the music was suddenly turned down. He looked up to see his mother coming in the room with him, and she was talking. Since his ears were still ringing from when the thing had been loud, he had to ask her to repeat herself.

"Why do you have a phone when you're not answering it?" He told her that he never had his phone on him when he was working. "Then you're going to have to find a different way of hearing when I call you, Houston. I've been ringing you for the last hour. Have you heard what is going on in Cincinnati?"

"Why would I care about what is going on in a city three hours away?" She asked him where the television was. "I don't have one out here. Just tell me, Mom. You have me nervous now."

"Justice and Arnold just went under. Mike Arnold—you know him, correct?" Houston nodded as his mom continued. "Mike has been arrested for tax fraud. They've got him on a lot of other charges too. Trafficking. Drugs. Prostitution. The man has a wife and children with two mistresses around town too."

"Lucky man." Mom smacked him upside the head. "You know that I'm a grown man, right?"

"Then start acting like it." Houston kissed her on the cheek and asked her if she wanted some tea to calm her nerves. "Yes, I think I do. Oh Houston, I'm sorry I took it out on you, but that man. Why do I just now have a memory of you and him having a huge falling out when you were in college?"

"We did. Over his now wife, Shasta." Mom asked if she'd been his mate. "No, it wasn't like that. He was dating Shasta, and told me it was getting very serious. Then an hour or so later I find him feeling up some other woman. He said that it was all fun and games."

"I guess he never changed his ways much."

Houston brewed his mom a cup of tea and one for himself. He loved hot tea, but wasn't so fond of cold tea. But Houston could drink gallons of water without pausing to go to the bathroom. He simply loved the cold clean taste of it.

"What do you suppose is going to happen to Shasta now? I mean, they have two little boys." His mom seemed genuinely concerned.

"I don't know. But I'd not get too worried about her. She's like a cat. Shasta always lands on her feet. If she can't get whatever she wants by conventional means, she simply bullies a person into giving it to her." Mom asked him why he'd bothered about her and Mike then. "I've never been sure about that. As far back as I can remember, Shasta has been like that. Her parents are about the nicest people you could ever want to meet. Mister's name is Blake Justice, and his wife is Trudy. I think there was another kid, but I never saw it. Why were you so hyped up about me seeing this, Mom?"

"I haven't any idea now. For some reason I had it in my head that you and Mike were friends. I thought that you'd be sad to hear about him." Houston hugged her, and then thanked his mom for caring about him. "I guess I didn't want you to find out about it later when you overheard something. Rogen is looking into things too. She was, I guess, before it came out in the papers."

"You didn't ask her about it, did you?" Mom told him that she wasn't insane. "Yes, well, she can be a bit protective of her work. Anna is doing a good job working with her, did

169

you hear that?"

"I did. But I hate that they had to delay their trip for it. I think that Morgan was planning this big to do with her and the kids." Houston had heard that too, but he was sure that Morgan was a big boy and could make other plans with his family. "Houston, can I ask you a personal question?"

"You can. But you'd better be prepared for the answer." She smiled at him. "Mom, I don't like that look. What are you stewing up in that beautiful mind of yours?"

"Oh, nothing like that. Trust me when I tell you, I'm never setting you up again." He said that he hoped not. "What I wanted to ask you is, are you making enough money at this? I want you to be happy. I do more than anything, but I don't want you to starve either. Or your mate to starve when she comes. If you ever come out of here, that is. How long do you work at this every day?"

"Not as much as my agent wants me to. And yes, I make very good money at playing in the mud." He got up to get his last commission check. He wasn't bragging, never that, but he also didn't want her to worry about him. "I got that for a three day showing that I didn't even have to attend. It took me about a year to get that much done, and another month for me to get things boxed up and shipped overseas."

"Oh my goodness, Houston. And you just let it lay on top of your microwave? What if you were robbed?" He asked her if she would think to look there for a check. "I guess not. You should be more careful with them."

"I will. There are two more of them about that size over there." He sipped his tea when she laughed. She more than likely thought that he wasn't serous, but he was. In fact, there were a total of four commission checks there that he'd not gotten around to taking to the bank yet.

When his mom left him, he dumped out the last of the tea and went back to work. He was working on things for next spring that he wanted to put together. He was forever a few seasons ahead of everyone else.

After closing up his shop later that night, he stood in the yard and stripped down to his bare skin. He so loved to run in the woods in the dark, and this was the perfect night to do it. There was a nice breeze in the air, the smell of the heat of the summer, as well as the flowers in the undergrowth of the trees.

Running as his cat was magnificent. Nothing bothered him. There wasn't anything in the trees that was bigger than him. And since he'd been a child, no one had ever been hunting on the land that his family had owned. Even running full out, he had time to admire everything around him.

Seeing his dad out in the yard made him smile. Dad didn't run as much as he used to. He would shift, come out by the stream that ran behind both their homes, and hide from Mom. Most of the time, however, Dad would take a nap and watch nature. It was where he'd gotten the need to have stillness around him when he was out here.

Mom mad at you? Dad asked him what he'd heard. *Nothing. But I've not seen you out here in a while, and I was concerned that you'd made her mad at you again.*

Not this time. I don't think, anyway. What are you doing out so late? He told him that he'd been working and decided that he needed a run. *Me too. I'm resting. I didn't remember you boys being as much work as these grandkids are. I surely do love them, but boy, they're almost too much for this old man.*

You're not an old man. And just wait until those girls of

171

Morgan's start dating. Dad growled at him. *Well, it is going to happen, you know.*

I do, but I'm not going to think about that right now. They sat there in the silence for a little while. *You ready to find your mate? I asked the others, and I thought for sure they were going to kick me to the curb. You gonna do that too?*

No. I'm as ready as a man can be for the unknown. Dad told him that was a good way to look at it. *Thanks. I will try my best to be open minded and a good mate. All of which will go down the tubes if she's anything at all like the other two are.*

Dad was laughing when they heard the sound of breaking branches in the forest. Neither of them moved, but watched everything around them. Nothing was making a sound. The crickets had stopped their calls, and the breeze had dried up like his mouth did right now.

The man staggered toward where they were. Houston was sure that he'd not seen either of them yet, but he wasn't taking any chances. Even from where they were sitting, Houston could smell the scent of fresh blood. As soon as the man fell, Houston and his dad took off for his studio. They'd help him, but only as men. Dad called the police as soon as he was dressed. Houston was just glad that he had an extra set of clothing for his dad to pull on.

Chapter 12

Morgan rolled to his back, and was thrilled beyond words that Anna was still in bed too. This thing of having nannies all the time was working out better for them. Now they were both getting the much needed rest that they needed.

They had tried for two weeks to do it all by themselves. Getting up for three children in the middle of the night was hard, especially when the girls were wearing different sized diapers than Eddie. Not to mention how much more they ate than their brother. Twice, before they had nannies, he'd put the wrong diaper on Eddie, and that had ended in disaster.

Rolling over to kiss Anna awake, he moaned when she wrapped her hand around his cock and squeezed him. She looked at him and smiled.

"I was going to jump your bones." He said she could still do that. "In a minute. I'm enjoying the way that you fit into my hand. Don't get me wrong—I love the way you fit inside of me too. But holding you like this, I can imagine you filling me up with it."

"I can do that too." Letting him go, she rolled him to his back and sat over him. His cock was right between her nether lips and she was soaking him. She rolled her body over him as she circled his crown with her fingers. "You keep that up and play time will be over shortly."

"You say that all the time, when we both know that you'll be ready to go ten minutes after you come. I've never been with anyone that bounces back as quickly as you do." He told her to hush about other men. "Yes, my lord. I want to feel you inside of me. I love it when you take me so slowly that it's like you simmer me until I'm tender, then you fuck me hard."

"Anna, honey, you're going to have to ride me before I come all over both of us." Anna moved. As he was reaching for her, she moved down his body until not only was her mouth doing wonderful things to his navel, but her hands were treating his skin like she was kneading dough. "Take me into your mouth. Please? I need to feel your heat there."

It was like a cool breeze blew over his cock for a second, then he was being heated to temperatures that made his head spin and his eyes roll to the back of his head. It was everything that he could do not to let go and fill her mouth with his cum.

Anna teased him, made him suffer in ways that sweat broke out on his body until he was soaked through. One second he was enjoying himself, loving what she was doing to him and his cock, and the next he was begging for her to release him, to let his cock go so that he could come.

Every part of his body enjoyed the way that she licked and sucked at him. His balls were abused, then pampered. Even his ass was massaged thoroughly. All the time she was doing these things to his body, he held onto his screams so as not to wake everyone in the state. Morgan wanted to scream about his pleasure. Tell the world that he was having more fun, more agony than any human or beast could stand.

When she finally moved up his body, the abuse/pleasure didn't stop. She bit him on his ribs. Licked his nipples until they were hard as stone and as painful as his cock was. Anna slid over his cock and he came. There was no holding back from it. That was what he needed, craved for her to give him. A place, a home for him to release all that he was inside of the woman that he loved.

Rolling her to her back, he took her hard. Pounding her through her own pleasure was making him fill again, his cock and balls painfully full. When Anna bit down on his shoulder and came, it was all he could do not to shift and bite her too.

Morgan had never seen stars when he came. Never felt the release of his cum from the top of his head to his feet. It was like an explosion that took his breath and heartbeat from him. Even his blood seemed to stop flowing to the rest of his body so that all his focus, all his energy, was used to fill Anna, his one true love, once again.

Then Morgan felt like he simply ceased to be. Releasing as he had, he was sure that he'd killed himself. Death by pleasure.

When he woke, he raised his head up to see where Anna was. The startling pain took his breath away. Even to move his arms to see if he'd hurt his head was too much. Every part of his body, including his ears, seemed to have been stretched to the point of pain. Laughing at himself, staggering to the shower, he reached out for Anna to see where she was.

I'm in the kitchen making breakfast for the girls. Eddie has had his breakfast, and is happily sleeping in his seat. I thought you were dead there for a little while. She laughed when he told her that he thought he had been. *Your mom will be here in about ten minutes. I was going to wake you if you weren't up by that time. Are you all right?*

I don't know, to be honest. How are you feeling? She said she felt fucking fantastic. *Of course you are. Christ, that was by far the best sex I've ever had in all my years. And if we do that ever again, I will be dead. That, my dear wife, is precisely why women live longer than men. You kill us with pleasure.*

Hurrying now so that he could see her before she left with his mom, he was downstairs when his mom came into the kitchen with them. She was already fussing at Rogen, who sat down in one of the chairs and begged for some tea. Anna was laughing as she poured her a cup, and told her that she needed to not stay up so late.

"I was in bed at a decent time, believe it or not. Then Jimmy wouldn't sleep in his bed, so he slept between us. I was terrified that I was going to roll over on him and smash him or something. I actually thought about going to get into his crib to sleep. How the fuck do you do this with three of them?" Morgan told her that Marie and Renee slept through the night. "Fucking bastards. I hate you both."

By the time the women were ready to leave, Lisha had joined them. She had arrived late yesterday afternoon, tanned and happy. Jamie was going to hang out with the men and the babies. Thatcher was at the hospital in surgery and would join them later. Dad showed up about the time a second pot of tea was set up to brew.

"I tell you what, Morgan. When Meggie asked me if I knew where they were going so that I could bring the trucks if they needed them, it scared me, not just a little either." Morgan laughed and poured his dad some tea. "She has her eye on one of them large entertainment centers. It's a massive thing too. Solid oak, so you know it'll be as heavy as it looks. I hope that they are outbid on it. I surely do."

"You know that they'll get it simply because you don't want to move it. But we'll all be there for you, Dad. Cheering you on as you move it to the truck." Dad glared at him. Morgan was feeling better now that he was moving around more. "I tell you what. If they buy too much, we'll just have a moving crew come in and move it for you. That should stop Mom from getting too much."

"No it won't, and you well know that. She'll just think she needs to get her money's worth and buy more."

They were both laughing when the rest of them joined them in the kitchen. The cook, Miss Penny, had arrived by then, and was ready to fix them all a hardy breakfast. Thatcher called to tell them that he was finished up. When Morgan told him that they were having breakfast, Thatcher decided to skip having a meal at the hospital and join them. Morgan was looking forward to having them all over today. It had been much too long since they'd had a guy's day together.

Since there wasn't any game on to watch yet, they found themselves sitting in the living room watching action movies. Jamie was having the most fun of all of them because he had never seen any. Morgan wondered if that was a good thing or bad, but they had fun, so he would take the hit if Rogen got mad. Besides, Thatcher was her mate, and he would take the biggest hit, like literally a hit from Rogen, if it came to that.

The kids, including Jimmy, played in the room with them, and he laughed when Dad ended up with all four of them in his lap sound asleep. It was the best picture he'd ever taken of his dad, and he was going to have it enlarged and hung in the kids' rooms. Morgan sent it to his mom, who sent him back a teary face emoji.

Anna called him just as they were eating subs that Dawson had gone to get for them. She was in a tizzy, and he felt his cat run along his skin. Then he laughed. Morgan laughed so hard that he had to sit down so as not to fall over.

"I don't think this is the least big funny, you fucking moron. I didn't stop. Your mother, of course, is hysterical. And Rogen is on the ground laughing too. This is not funny." He told her that it was. "You have no idea how much I wanted them for the girls, Morgan. I cannot wait for you to see it. It's so beautiful that I can hardly stand to walk away from it."

She had managed to not only get them a set of bunkbeds made of maple, but two dressers with mirrors, as well as trunks, to match the set. There was a rocking chair, she told him, as well as two computer desks that went with it. Anna had gotten a deal of a lifetime, he was sure, because no one wanted to move it.

"So, how much did you pay for this deal of a lifetime, love? I'm sure that you did good, or Mom wouldn't be laughing at you." Anna told him that she'd been laughing at her all morning so far. "She means well, I'm sure."

"I'm not. I paid a whole fifty dollars for the entire set." That made him stop laughing, and he asked her if she was sure. "Yes, I'm sure. Morgan, are you mad at me for doing this?"

"Hell no, I'm not. Honey, that's amazing. Fifty bucks for the girls' room? Hell, I would have paid more if I had been there. And I can see the trunks being used for all kinds of treasures for them. Do you think that whoever had it in the first place had twins too?" She told him that they had twin boys, but she didn't think that it would matter. "No, this is amazing. Are you having fun?"

"I am, as a matter of fact. I have to go. There is another thing that I want to get for Eddie. It's a rocking horse. The lady that was looking at it with me already told me she was going to only pay twenty bucks for it. Meggie said that it was worth more than that, so I'm going to go there now." He told her that he loved her. "I love you too. Why didn't you ever tell me how much fun these were?"

After she hung up, he told them what she'd gotten. His brothers were so impressed that they said they'd help him move it into the room they'd been thinking to put the girls in. He told them that they were working on the room now, to get it painted and the carpet pulled up and the floor sanded down.

Within minutes the television was off, the kids were put in playpens, and they hit the room with full force. Even Dad woke up enough to go and borrow a sander to get the floor finished before the women returned with their items. Morgan loved his family more in that moment than he thought he ever had.

~*~

Tru, dressed as a doctor, made her way through the hospital. Twice she was asked a question, and was able to answer it. She even, to make herself look the part, stopped in the ER department to assist with a patient. All her knowledge seemed to be coming in handy with this one.

The man that she was after was in surgery for another hour or so. Moving through the hospital, she observed a great many things that she was impressed by. There was enough staff on duty that it made her think that she wouldn't mind being here if she was hurt again. Not to mention, she heard a great deal about the doctors that volunteered their time and knowledge at local schools and clinics.

Her cell going off made her pause long enough to look at it, but not answer. She knew what was going on with her sister's husband. Mike had been one of the many projects that she'd been working on simultaneously with this one. He'd been bad news since high school. The man had not improved as he'd gotten older, either. Today had been in the works for nearly a year. Tru was sorry for her sister, but not enough to stop doing what she did.

Dad knew some of what was going on, but not Tru's part in Mike's fall from grace, if he was ever there. He'd been approached by her boss and asked to help out. Tru was thrilled to have found out that not only was her dad willing to help the Feds, but he'd been looking into things for himself. Good old Dad had been her inspiration in pursuing her career as an undercover agent for the government.

He might not have been all that happy with her career choice. In fact, she was positive that he'd hate it. She'd been tortured, shot, and jailed so many times in her job that he would have had her committed for doing something that she loved. Helping with bad guys was a good job. It really sucked that there were so many of them.

Tru helped in the ER with a patient that had been in a car accident. Setting his leg and admitting him raised no questions. Her cover, filling in for a doctor who was on vacation, was perfect. The doctor in question had won a two week trip to Hawaii two days ago, and had to take it now. Now all she had to do was finish the job that had been started when the man in surgery had been shot and not killed, as he should have been.

The man, Agent Allen DeLong, had been selling information to other countries for the past six months. She'd only been made aware of it yesterday when she'd been told to come here and finish up. The man who she was replacing was now dead — DeLong had killed him when he'd been shot himself.

Tru didn't care for being clean up man. She knew that all kinds of things could go wrong with what she was doing. Lucky for her, she had an eidetic memory, and had read as many books as she could on a plethora of subjects and languages that she could blend in better than most agents. Lucky for Tru too, no one believed that what she could do was a real thing.

As soon as she was aware that DeLong was out of surgery, she made her way up to the second floor after helping with one more victim. She knew exactly what she had to do and when to do it. The trouble was, getting to him before anyone else did. Her phone went off again, and this time she didn't bother looking to see who it was.

Shasta would have to deal with the outcome of what was going down on her own. Tru had told her, over and over, not to marry Mike. She'd even suggested, several times, that he was having numerous affairs. Not only did she not care about that, so long as she had the picture perfect lifestyle for others to see, Shasta was willingly blinded by all the signs that Tru set out for her to find.

Sneaking into the room where Delong was recovering, she was glad to see that he was alone. The cameras in here had been dealt with by the company, and she walked to the bed that he was in. Delong never opened his eyes when she injected him with aconite, or wolfbane, right into his IV.

It would appear that he had a heart attack. His heart would race until it just stopped beating. Tru was out of the room even before the crash cart was there to try and save him. The lab coat that she had on helped her leave the place unnoticed.

There would be no fingerprints to trace—she had none. No DNA to try and gather, Tru was always careful of that. And thanks to the man working the computers in the building, on loan too from the government, no one would ever have a picture of her in the ER or the recovery room.

Making her way down the hall, she saw a familiar face. Lowering her head so as not to be recognized, the pain in her belly nearly took her to the floor. The man that shot her was gone by the time she was able to turn around.

Looking down at her hand, she could see that she was bleeding badly from a wound in her belly. It was a gunshot wound that wouldn't be fixed with duct tape, like she usually used until she could get someplace to get herself fixed up. Staggering to the nurses' station, she pulled out her cell phone before it was too late for her.

"Number one seven four eight. Down. Last location." She closed her eyes, wondering where the answering beep was. Just when she was ready to admit that she wasn't going to get it, the answering beeps made her weep a little. "Agent down. Repeat, agent down."

Nurses were moving much too fast for her dizziness, so she closed her eyes. Opening the phone, she took out the battery and the sim card and busted the phone. Christ, she needed to stay aware for just a few more minutes. She was also worried about her Charlie now, and if he would have someone take care of him if she was hurt.

The phone ringing at the nurses' desk had her hanging on for just a few moments longer. More time than she thought that she had.

"Are you…? Let me get this right. Are you one seven four eight?" Tru nodded. "I'm to call Dr. Robinson to operate on you. I'm to ask you if you need anything."

"No." A very large man was coming down the hall. Staggering a little more, she felt herself being lifted up into his arms. "Robinson?"

"Yes." She was laid down and they started to work on her—putting in an IV, taking her temp, asking her questions that she couldn't answer—or rather wouldn't. "I'm to tell you that zero zero three two is on her way."

She couldn't let the drugs take her under until she met with the other agent. Robinson seemed to know this, and had all activity stop regarding putting her under for the surgery to remove the bullet. Tru knew that she was in deep shit here because of two things. She was bleeding badly, and Tru had been shot by another agent.

"Agent, can you hear me?" Prying her eyes open, she looked at the legendary Rogen Hall. Tru had only seen pictures of her. They didn't do the woman justice. "Agent?"

"Have kit." The things she had on her were handed over to Rogen. She asked her if she knew who had shot her. "Yes. Agent twelve fifty-three. Assignment is complete."

Tru could no longer keep her eyes open. If she were to die right now, which she thought was a very good possibility, her family would never know what she was doing here. Her death would be written off as a car accident, just the way she'd planned for it to look. No one would acknowledge her,

her job, or what she had been doing here. Tru was nothing more than a fart in the wind as far as most of the world would know.

~*~

Rogen didn't leave the hospital as she should have done. Nor did she take care that the phone calls were made that were needed so that the woman in the operating room would know that she'd not only completed her job, but that she'd not given any information to anyone about it. The kit in her hand, the one that the woman had given her, not only carried a used syringe, but also enough aconite to kill several large men in a matter of seconds.

That didn't bother her. What did bother her, and the reason that Rogen hadn't called it in, was that she'd been shot by one of her kind. Another agent had tried to kill her. May have, according to Thatcher.

Sitting in his office, waiting for Thatcher to tell her if the woman lived, Rogen looked out the window and tried to think. In this hospital someone was dead. A person that the young woman would have killed to have completed her assignment. Instead of calling anyone that might well have the answers to the million and one questions going around in her head, she called Patrick.

Rogen knew that he was on vacation. It was actually his honeymoon, but no one but her and Thatcher knew that. Winnie James, one of her best friends and colleagues, had married him the day before yesterday. As soon as Patrick answered, she knew that someone had contacted him about what was going on in their little town.

"Are you on a secure line?" She told him that she was forever when talking to him. "Good. You have in your hospital a woman by the name of Trudy Justice. She's named after her mother, I guess. Anyway, Tru—she goes by that, believe it or not…Tru. I take it that someone contacted you about her. Are you to kill her? If you were told that, don't. She's about as valuable as you are, Rogen."

Rogen told him what she knew. He asked her if anyone else know that she'd been shot by another agent. Now Rogen was beginning to worry.

"No. That's why I called you. Nothing about this is making me all warm and fuzzy. You know me well enough to know that very little makes me feel that way, but there is something very hinky about this." Patrick told her she was a smart cookie. "So, are you going to tell me what's going on, or do I have to go where you are and beat it out of you?"

"She's an agent, as you're aware, that goes in and cleans up messes that might occur. The target that she had this morning was a man by the name of Allan DeLong. He was working doubles with another country for a little while now. His body was recovered—"

"On our land this morning." Patrick said that was right. "Thatcher worked on him. It'll really piss him off when he finds out that he's dead. I have to at least give him something for this. It really does bother him to lose one."

"You know that we trust him as much as we do you. Just between you two, however, it's going to look like he suffered a heart attack. Unless someone is looking for aconite, they're not going to find it. So he'll be in the clear." Rogen thanked him. "Justice was sent in to finish up the job that another agent, dead as well, was to have taken care of yesterday. We only found out about this, I guess, when his body turned up in Thatcher's operating room."

"What do you want me to do about Justice? You know as well as I do that we can make her death very public so that they think they got their man." Patrick said it was already taken care of. The people in the operating room with Thatcher were going to help him. "Where do I take her after this? And those helping him—who hired them? You or the other agent's guy?"

It was barely a second before he started cursing. Rogen stood up just as Patrick stopped cursing and told her what she needed to do.

"Check on Thatcher. Mother fuck, I never thought of that. Also, she has a dog. A monster of a thing. You'll have to go and get it for her."

She was leaving Thatcher's office when she thought of something else. Telling Patrick, he told her that if things went south for Thatcher, he'd call in a clean-up crew.

"I have to go. I'm standing right outside the operating room right now. Just send the crew, Patrick. I don't want this to linger around too much if there is need for the crew." He said to consider them there. "I owe you."

When she put her phone in her pocket, she realized that she was going to have to find the one that Justice had. Just as she was thinking of the trash cans between here and recovery, one of the nurses pulled out a handgun with a silencer on it. She never got to pull the trigger.

Chapter 13

Thatcher was trying his best not to freak out. All he could think about was that someone had planned to kill him. It hadn't had a thing to do with him being married to Rogen, either. Only that he'd been in the wrong place at the wrong time.

There had been three people, two nurses and an anesthesiologist, with him in the operating room. One of the nurses was dead, the other was in Rogen's custody. The anesthesiologist had committed suicide by arsenic just before Rogen was able to arrest him.

Thatcher's hands were still shaking when Rogen asked him if he was all right. "No, I'm not fucking all right." She kissed him on the mouth. "That helps, but it doesn't negate the fact that someone was willing to put a bullet in my head because I was called in to help a patient that needed me."

"I'm sorry. If I hadn't called Patrick to talk to him, it would have been too late." Thatcher told her that she wasn't helping at all. "I'm sorry, honey. I truly am. But you'll be

187

happy to know that we know who the killer was. Who killed Mr. DeLong, as well. Agent Justice is going to be hanging out at our house until we can make sure that she's safe."

"I signed her death certificate." Rogen kissed him again. "Rogen, I'm sure that you're aware of this, but you need to explain more and try to distract me less. All right? Someone just tried to kill me."

"Okay." Rogen took him to his office and closed and locked the door. When she sat on the corner of his desk closest to him, Thatcher leaned into her so that he'd hear whatever she had to say to him. "Tru Justice, that's her name, is the woman that you saved. She's like, really important to the government. She has an eidetic memory. Do you know what that is?"

"Yes, but that isn't a real thing." She only nodded at him. "Are you telling me that she remembers every sound, word, and language she hears? That's not possible—you know that, right?"

"It is for her. Case in point, she read books on what a doctor does in his everyday work. Then she looked up each of those procedures to see exactly how to do them. Then, Patrick told me, she read up on more things, emergency things to do, so that she'd blend into coming here for this job. Justice also speaks every language that can be used, even a couple of dead ones. She did a stint as a race car driver. Can fly a plane as well as a helicopter." Thatcher was impressed. If any of that was true. "Thatcher, she worked in your emergency room for over three hours waiting for you to get out of surgery for DeLong. And she did it flawlessly."

"Okay, she's good. But why did someone shoot her?" Rogen said that they were working on that. "As in you know and need more information, or you don't know and are starting from scratch?"

"Both. We know who shot her, but we can't do shit about it because — well, he's dead. I didn't do it, but whoever sent him here to take care of her." Thatcher asked if that was the unknown. "That, and it's someone that works with Patrick and me."

Now that scared him more. To have someone right in the government working to kill off an agent…well, that was something that would keep him up at nights. Thatcher asked her what she needed from him.

"Two things. First of all, you are going to quit your job sooner rather than later. I can't watch over you here when I can't be in the operating room with you. The second thing is, and this wasn't my call, the agencies are paying to have yours and Dawson's building finished by the end of the week. They're going to use you both, if you agree, as their emergency room for agents and the like that can get to you faster than back to home. They want that up and running as soon as possible. You can turn them down, but I'd not. They'll be able to have a staff on board with you that will keep you both safer than I can, not to mention all your patients. In additional, they'll pay all the insurance for both you and Dawson."

"Christ, they certainly make it hard to turn down, don't they?" She told him that she loved him. "Are you telling me that because there is more?"

"I do love you, dumbass, but there is more." He asked her if it could wait until he processed what he already had heard. "I suppose, but it's nothing bad."

"All right, tell me. I can handle one more thing, I guess." Instead of answering him as he thought that she would,

Rogen took his hand into hers and put it on her belly. He felt the movement almost as soon as he touched her. "That's our baby."

"Yes." She was grinning like he was sure that he was. "I felt it earlier when I was talking to Patrick the second time, but I didn't know what it was. It just occurred to me that it's our baby moving, and I couldn't wait to share with you."

Thatcher leaned down and put his head on their child. He could feel the fluttering that was there, feeling it like the baby was telling him that it was there to distract him even more. Pulling up her shirt, he kissed the mound and looked up at Rogen.

"I love you so very much." She kissed him again, this time longer and with more heat. "I can't wait to hold it. Jimmy will love having a sibling, don't you think?"

"I do. And I wasn't distracting you so much as I was bubbling over with the need to tell you, and I thought that this would be a great way to make you realize that things could be a lot worse." He nodded, still holding her belly in his larger hands. "Thatcher, I'm so happy you pissed me off enough to fall in love with you."

"Forever the romantic." She laughed and told him that she had to get back to work. There were things still going on. "I'll have to talk to Dawson about the other thing."

"I hope he says yes. They started on the building about an hour ago." She skipped away and Thatcher had to laugh. His wife was going to drive him insane, but he loved her anyway.

Dawson was in his office in the ER. He knew that he'd been stressing out about this place, but he had a feeling that today was about all he could handle. The new administrators had sent down another memo, a memo that was about four pages long, on things that were going to be changing soon. Most of it having to do with nurses and how they were going to be treated from now on.

"Did you read this shit?" Thatcher told him that he'd only seen the topic. "Yes, well, let me read you a few lines of this bullshit. You'd think, oh good. Nurses are going to be treated better. Get a raise. Or, I don't know, they're going to have more help. No. It's nothing like that at all. They want them to wear their own clothing in here to save costs and make them more friendly looking to the patients. Can you fucking imagine the germs that we'll be dealing with because of that? Everyday clothing my ass. Next they'll tell us that they should wear open toe shoes so that they'll get whatever is all over the floor too. Fuckers."

"When is your notice up?" Dawson eyed him. "What if I told you that the building that we're working on will be finished up by the end of the week? That we will have partners that will not only pay our medical insurance, but also help us out with staffing?"

"Who?" He told him what Rogen had told him. "When can we start? I have to tell you, Thatcher, I'm an inch away from just walking. And in answer to your question, my notice was up yesterday. I'm helping out because 'they're still looking for the perfect fit,' they told me."

"I'll help you pack up." In an hour, not only did they have Dawson packed up, but his office was emptied as well. Thatcher had packed his stuff up a couple of days ago, but hadn't had the time to take it out. The two of them walked out together as his notice, like his brother's, had been over yesterday.

Driving toward the offices, he told him everything that he

could concerning what was going on around them. Thatcher didn't mention the murder attempt on him. Nor did he say anything about their guests in one of the upstairs bedrooms. Charlie hadn't put up a bit of fuss once they got him into the car. It was like he didn't care at all that a cat was taking him to his master.

Pulling into the parking lot that was going to serve as their new offices, both of them just sat there and stared at the work already finished in the place.

"Did you know that we were going to paint it blue?" Thatcher said that it wouldn't have been his first choice, but he did like it. "Me too. Sort of cozy looking, I guess. There's a lot of equipment going in the back, did you see that?"

He hadn't, so they made their way back there. Thatcher didn't notice that they'd had loading docks before, but apparently they had them now. The buildings, one on either side of them, were being renovated too. While he didn't know they were for sale before, he supposed they could always find something to use them for.

"Are you by chance the Doctors Robinson?" Both he and Dawson nodded. "I'm the agent in charge of the work being done. Your wife said that she sent you a picture of me so that you could talk to me. I'm only here to talk about the buildings."

Thatcher pulled out his phone and saw the note attached to it. If this wasn't the man, she said for him to kill him. He had no idea how he was going to pull that off, but he was glad that it was who was in the picture. His name was Cody Wayne.

Dawson was talking to Cody about the other two buildings and why they were being fixed up too. Thatcher caught up with the two of them as they entered the building on the right of their offices.

"These will be for you to use for regular patients that will need an overnight stay. Everything in these rooms, eighteen in all, will have all the state of the art equipment that the hospital should have." Dawson said they thought that the hospital was far behind in that. "They are. In addition to that, there will be two cameras in each of the rooms that will be monitored at all times. Just to make sure that the people you have in here are actually who you think they are."

Dawson looked a little confused, but Thatcher could help him later with that. Both of them were very impressed at how far they'd come in getting things ready, as well as the way they had it laid out. Cody told them that they'd had a lot of practice in setting these sorts of things up.

When he took them to the other building, Thatcher noticed that not only wasn't there any sort of identification on the building, but you had to have a swipe card and a code to get into the place.

"I'll set that up for you as soon as we have a look around. It's my understanding that you're aware of the agent already here." Thatcher said that he was, and that he'd explain that to his brother later. "Good. No one but agents will ever use this building. You aren't to use it for anyone else than that, or they'll be shot. I'm not joking here. We cannot have anyone knowing who these people are, ever."

Nodding to tell him that they understood, Thatcher put his badge around his neck as Cody explained about them. They'd be able to get into any of the three buildings with them, but no one else would. The staff in here were only people that were trusted by the agencies that were using the building.

This building, like the other, was all up to date. The only difference was this one had a full pharmacy in the lower levels that had to be swiped into as well. The pharmacists, they were told, would be there full time for both places if it came to that.

When they were ready to leave, after Thatcher checked on Justice, they sat in the parking lot and said nothing for several minutes. Thatcher explained to Dawson everything that was going on with the woman, but about the rest, he was just as stunned as his brother was. Finally, Dawson spoke.

"I'm not sure if I should be thrilled or scared out of my mind with this." Thatcher said he was feeling that too. "We'll be paid well, I'm assuming."

"I didn't ask." Dawson said that he was grasping for straws right now. "I know what you mean there as well. It's like we've been handed an endless supply of all day suckers, and I'm waiting for someone to tell me it was a joke."

Dawson nodded. Taking him home again, they neither said much and nothing at all about the new digs. He was sure that they'd both have questions tomorrow, but for now it was too overwhelming to nail any one of them down.

~*~

Tru woke up and looked around the room she was in. Nothing was anything that she remembered, but she did know that she was in some sort of hospital. If she didn't miss her bet, she was in some kind of hospital that was unknown to anyone but a very few. Tru didn't even know what state or even what country she was in at the moment.

The nurse that came to where she was looking wasn't like any other nurse that she'd seen in a hospital. She was carrying a gun, cuffs, and a stethoscope. Strange and surreal, but necessary for who Tru worked for.

"Agent, do you need anything for pain?" Shaking her head, Tru asked her if there was anything that she could tell her. "No, I'm afraid not. At least not about the situation. I can tell you that you're under the care of Doctor Thatcher Robinson. He is, along with his brother, Doctor Dawson Robinson, taking care of you and your wound. You have something for pain should you want it, and you can have sips of water until they say differently."

All she wanted, she told her, was to rest. After the nurse said that she would call the doctor to tell them she was awake, Tru closed her eyes. Then she remembered that she should have asked her the date.

When she woke again, not realizing that she'd fallen asleep, the man sitting in the chair across from her was someone that she knew. Agent Donaldson was looking through a file and had a kit, a death kit they all called them, sitting beside him.

"Is that for me?" Startled, he looked at her, confused. Then he put his hand over the kit. "Are you here to end my life?"

"Good heavens no. As far as I'm concerned, you're a hero. A dead one to most of the agency, but a hero all the same." She asked about her sister. "Shasta is not aware of anything having to do with you. Nor are your parents."

"Have you caught up with her husband yet?" He just smiled at her. "Sorry, force of habit to know it all at once. Am I all right?"

"Yes. You had the best surgeon we know. You're set up here because of him too." So she was still in Ohio. "I'm here to update you on a few things that I can. Also to get a few questions answered that we're not sure of. Delong, as you know, is dead. No one suspected a thing, and he was quietly buried a week ago. In the event you don't know, you've been

195

here for about ten days, give or take a few hours."

There wasn't any reason for her to think about how long that had been and what she might have missed. She was still alive, and that was all that mattered at this point. There wasn't any point in getting all worked up over something that she couldn't change or do anything about.

Patrick asked her the questions, all of which she had the answers to. Where was the phone that she'd used to call in? In the kit that she'd given agent Hall. Did anyone recognize her before or after? Tru told him how the shooter knew her and she him. He told her that he too was dead, but they were working on who might have given him the order to kill her.

"What happens to me now? If I can ask." He sighed, and she was sure that he was going to tell her that she was finished. "I'm not ready to be put out to pasture yet."

"I should hope not. No, but you will have to remain dead until we can figure out what agency or who personally wanted you dead. The person that shot you, he was there for one thing and one thing only. To take you out." Tru asked him how he could be so sure. "No one but you and your handler, my new wife, knew what you were there for. So how he figured out you'd be there, we're still working on. You'll be working behind the scenes until we have it."

"I see." She didn't like to be behind anyone or anything, but would cooperate because she loved what she did that much. He told her who she'd be working with. "No, you must have that wrong. Agent Hall is the best there is, and from what I've been told no more needs a helper than I do."

"Well, she will on this. And with your other skills, I think that she'll use you a great deal after this." He laughed a little before continuing. "She's married too, I should tell you. Her name is now Rogen Robinson."

That took a second or two to sink in. When she got it, Tru just stared at him. Rogen was married to one of her doctors? While she might not know the woman personally, she had heard enough stories about her to know that she was as hard as nails, and ate them for every meal. And if you pissed her off, you'd be as dead as…well, you'd just never be heard from or found again kind of dead.

Tru never thought that the woman would find someone to love, much less put up with her, but she had a kid too? Tru laid back on the bed and thought about that. She must really love the guy, and him a saint if this were a fact.

"Seems like getting married is an epidemic around here. I sure as fuck hope that I don't ever get it." Patrick laughed again. "Christ, do you have any idea what sort of person would find me loveable? No one, that's who. I don't even like myself most days. I can't imagine spending the rest of my life with someone. Much less having kids."

After he left her, giving her a clean phone and a gun to keep, she was helped from her bed and sat in a chair. It was painful as fuck, but at least with moving around a little, she didn't feel as druggy.

There were a great many things that she had to think about. Patrick had left her some newspapers to look over. They were from her hometown, so she was able to keep up with her sister without actually speaking to her. She was having as hard a time as Tru thought she would. And milking it just as badly.

The file that he'd been looking over was about Rogen and her family. He wanted her to be familiar with the family that she was going to be working with for a while, as well as know as much about them as possible, so if necessary, she could pass as a visiting cousin to Rogen. There were pictures of the family as well, and a bit on each of them. They were tigers.

It mattered little to her what people were. Gay, straight. Shifter or human. It didn't matter. If you fucked up, she would end your life without a second thought. But the Robinsons didn't seem to have any skeletons in their closet. Or they'd had their files so washed over by Rogen that they appeared that way.

Even as good as Rogen was, Tru wouldn't trust her right off. She didn't trust many people, and with good reason. To her everyone had a price. Even her sister did. When she'd married the man that would fill her needs as a perfect wife, she'd not taken into consideration what sort of man she was actually marrying. No matter how many people told her she'd be better off marrying anyone but him, she did so anyway. And now was paying the cost of it.

According to some paperwork she had, Shasta was broke. Not only had she had her accounts locked, but her household was going to be taken from her. The house, the cars, the fancy school, all gone because it had been paid for by her husband being a dumbass.

Tru thought about where she lived and laughed. Shasta was forever bitching how she'd never been to her home. Not to her, of course, but to her friends and Mom. It was a one bedroom imaginary home for her.

There was a mattress that laid on the floor. No food in the cabinets or the fridge, which Tru didn't even think had been plugged in for over a year. She kept nothing there because she was rarely there. No dishes, no pots and pans. She ate out if she had to be there, and her clothing was brought in by her and taken out the same way. Tru didn't even have a toothbrush that she left there.

It was a place, that was it. Not her home — she didn't have one. While she could drive a car, there wasn't one there either. She did own a Jeep, which was used more for getting her ass from point one to point two than anything else. By now she realized everything in her place would have been sanitized, given away, or burned, and no one would ever know that she had lived there.

Not that it mattered. There was nothing that pulled at her heartstrings, not even a book that she enjoyed reading. Tru was nothing, as she'd been called before, but a fart in the wind.

The armed nurse came in with a cell phone a few minutes after she made her way to the bathroom. Tru hurt, but the alternative was a great deal worse. Being dead gave you no pain, and she was going to enjoy her pain because she was still breathing.

"There is a call for you, Agent. It's Agent Hall." So the staff had no idea that Rogen was married. Good to know. "She asked that you close the door after I leave."

It was difficult to get up a second time, but when the door was closed, she realized why she'd been asked to close it and not the nurse. The thing had three locks on it, and the door itself was solid steel. Tru locked them all.

"Agent Justice."

Tru heard a baby gurgling before Rogen spoke. Her laughter, for some reason, brought a smile to her own face.

"Hey, this is Rogen. I guess you know that the two of us will be working together." She said that was what she'd been told. "Get the rod out of your ass, Agent. This will be good for us both if you work and play well with me."

"I don't work or play well with others, ma'am." Rogen laughed again. Tru heard a man's voice, then the baby noises getting further away. "I have been given a file on all your family. I've been studying it."

"I have one on you too, Tru. I'm betting that you know all about my family verbatim. But that won't do you a fucking nickel's worth of good if you're asked, and we both know that." She did. A file could have all kinds of information in it, but nothing about the people that she was to see. "I have a couple of tapes that I'd like for you to listen to. I've never used an interpreter before because the thing was already translated when I got it. But for some reason I think that this, what I have, is nothing about what I've been given."

"Is it verbal or written?" Rogen asked her if it mattered. "Not really. I can read and translate voice too. What language is it in?"

"Farsi. Can you understand that?" She said that she could and asked her to play it. "All right. But just to give you a heads up, as soon as you're able to piss by yourself, they're sending you to my home."

"I just pissed all by myself not an hour ago." The way that Rogen said it made her realize that not only couldn't Rogen read Farsi, she couldn't understand it either. So this wasn't a test of her skills as she thought it might be. Tru translated it word for word for Rogen. "Is that what you have there?"

"Not even close. They told me it was a recipe for some kind of cake or some shit like that." Tru asked her if she had the original or a copy. "I have a copy. Why do you ask?"

"I've been reading correspondence from this region before. I can tell where it's from by the dialect. If you had the original, I'm thinking that you'd have a bit more than just what is on the paperwork you have. Can you get it?" She asked her to hold on.

When she had it, Tru told her to get herself a heating pad and put it on high. When it was warm enough, she then told her to put the original on the heating pad and wait. She could hear her yelling about sneaky shit, and had to laugh. Rogen was easy to please, it seemed.

"Where the hell did you learn that shit?" Tru told her that she'd been doing this for a while now. "About as long as I have, I guess. You're going to be very helpful, Tru. I hope I can convince you to put down some roots here and stick around."

"I doubt it, ma'am. I'm not much into roots. I've seen what it does to people, and I'm not going to get myself shackled to anything unless it has a big cock, he's good in bed, and has enough education that I can have a conversation with him if I'm not fucking him—oh, and a cook. I want a cook that will give me shit when I want it, and home cooking when I want that too." Rogen said those weren't all that high of standards. "No. But there is one more thing that will never happen for me. I fucking will not, for as long as I have the power, marry anyone. I'm not going to be responsible for another living soul when I can barely care for myself."

"At one time, I thought that same thing. I got it all. Even a baby on the way." Tru congratulated her. "Also, if you call me ma'am one more time, you're not going to have to worry about your list. I'm going to kick your ass so badly that you'll wish for death simply because there is nothing left for you."

"There are many days that I already think there is nothing left for me." Tru had no idea why she shared that with Rogen.

But taking it back was impossible now, and she wasn't going to apologize for stating the truth. What was done was done.

"Tru, Thatcher is on his way to pick you up. He's bringing you here. There are a few things that you and I are going to work on as soon as you're up to it." She asked about her family. "As far as we're concerned right now, we are your family. But I understand that you have to extend your being gone from the others. You told them a couple of weeks, correct?"

"I did. I was leaving to get away from the news that was going down." Rogen asked her how much she had to do with that shit. Tru didn't answer. She was all of it, but if her boss wanted Rogen to know, she'd know. But Tru didn't work and tell. "I'll see you soon."

Before You Go...

HELP AN AUTHOR

write a review

THANK YOU!

Share your voice and help guide other readers to these wonderful books. Even if it's only a line or two your reviews help readers discover the author's books so they can continue creating stories that you'll love. Login to your favorite retailer and leave a review. Thank you.

AWARD WINNING, BESTSELLING AUTHOR

Kathi Barton, winner of the Pinnacle Book Achievement award as well as a best-selling author on Amazon and All Romance books, lives in Nashport, Ohio with her husband Paul. When not creating new worlds and romance, Kathi and her husband enjoy camping and going to auctions. She can also be seen at county fairs with her husband who is an artist and potter.

Her muse, a cross between Jimmy Stewart and Hugh Jackman, brings her stories to life for her readers in a way that has them coming back time and again for more. Her favorite genre is paranormal romance with a great deal of spice. You can visit Kathi online and drop her an email if you'd like. She loves hearing from her fans. aaronskiss@gmail.com.

Follow Kathi on her blog: http://kathisbartonauthor. blogspot.com/

Made in the USA
Coppell, TX
17 November 2019